CALLIE'S LAST DANCE

a Donovan Creed Novel - Volume 10
John Locke

TELEMACHUS PRESS

This is a work of fiction. All of the characters, names, incidents, organizations, and dialogue in this novel are either the products of the author's imagination or are used fictitiously.

CALLIE'S LAST DANCE
Copyright © 2012, 2013 John Locke. All rights reserved, including the right to reproduce this book, or portions thereof, in any form. No part of this text may be reproduced, transmitted, downloaded, decompiled, reverse engineered, or stored in or introduced into any information storage and retrieval system, in any form or by any means, whether electronic or mechanical without the express written permission of the author. The scanning, uploading, and distribution of this book via the Internet or via any other means without the permission of the author or publisher is illegal and punishable by law. Please purchase only authorized electronic editions and do not participate in or encourage electronic piracy of copyrighted materials.

The publisher does not have any control over and does not assume any responsibility for author or third-party websites or their content.

Cover designed by: Head of Zeus
http://www.headofzeus.com

Published by: Telemachus Press, LLC
http://www.telemachuspress.com

Visit the author's website:
http://www.donovancreed.com

ISBN: 978-1-938135-63-7

Printed in the United States of America

10 9 8 7 6 5 4 3 2 1

Personal Message from John Locke:

I love writing books! But what I love even more is hearing from readers. If you enjoyed this or any of my other books, it would mean the world to me if you'd send a short email to introduce yourself and say hi. I always personally respond to my readers.

I would also love to put you on my mailing list to receive notifications about future books, updates, and contests.

Please visit my website, http://www.DonovanCreed.com, so I can personally thank you for trying my books.

John Locke

New York Times Best Selling Author

8th Member of the Kindle Million Sales Club
(which includes James Patterson, Stieg Larsson, George R.R. Martin
and Lee Child, among others)

John Locke had 4 of the top 10 eBooks on
Amazon/Kindle at the same time, including #1 and #2!

...Had 6 of the top 20, and 8 books in the top 43 at the same time!

...Has written 19 books in three years in four separate genres,
all best-sellers!

...Has been published in numerous languages by many of the world's
most prestigious publishing houses!

Acknowledgments

Special thanks to loyal Donovan Creed fan Rick Kocan, a great guy, fellow Penn State fan, and neuroradiologist, who told me about a special MRI machine that could possibly benefit one of the characters in my book. Thanks also to my brother, Ricky, who devoted an entire day of his valuable time to help me make this book that much better, and to Claudia Jackson, of Telemachus Press, who works tirelessly for me, and goes into her "above and beyond" mode almost daily!

CALLIE'S
LAST DANCE

Prologue

RIDLEY'S WIFE, CONNIE, doesn't cheat very often, but when she does it's going to take place in room 316 at the Winston Parke Hotel in downtown Cincinnati.

Three-sixteen, because it's her lucky number.

Her date of birth.

March sixteenth.

Ridley knows this, he's followed her there several times.

While he strongly disapproves of Connie's extra-marital affair, the guy she's fucking is Tom Bell, the number two ranked mixed martial artist in the world. Ridley's no wimp, but Bell could kick Ridley's ass with one hand while fingering Connie with the other.

Which is why Ridley plans to kill them from a distance.

Ridley may not know martial arts, but as a commercial builder he knows a thing or two about concrete. For example, he knows concrete floors in modern hotels are usually eight inches thick and pre-stressed, while seventy-year-old floors, like those in the Winston Parke, are only four inches thick and composed of light-weight concrete.

Ridley also knows hand guns. He's collected them all his life. For example, he knows his Nitro Zeliska is the largest, most-powerful handgun in the world. Knows it fires a 900-grain, 600 round at 1,950 feet per second while producing a whopping 7,591 foot pounds of muzzle energy. He knows it set him back nearly twenty grand, plus forty bucks a bullet.

The Winston Parke lobby has a café on one side, a bank of glass elevators on the other. Ridley's sitting in the café, sipping his coffee, watching Connie and Tom Bell take an elevator to the third floor.

For Ridley, it's come full-circle.

He's the one who introduced Connie to room 316 years ago, when she was in design school. He's the one who wined, dined, and married her, the one who adored her, took care of her, and introduced her to society. He's the one who gave her the life of luxury, funded her home decorating business, showered her with gifts, took her places she'd never been ...

And this is how she pays him back.

Ridley stares at his coffee, trying to forget what he saw.

Tom, patting his wife's ass.

Connie, showing Tom the bedroom smile Ridley used to get.

He sighs.

What kind of wife would do him this way?

He knows the answer.

A younger one.

What it all comes down to, the younger wives want a guy on the side. You shower them with love, bring them all the way up the ladder of success, and get what in return?

Gratitude?

Loyalty?

No. What you get is attitude. After a few years of fucking you, they want to fuck what you're not.

Ridley's got it figured out. He'd say if you want to predict who your wife's gonna fuck, look for the guy who's nothing like you. If you're handsome, they'll fuck ugly. If you're ugly, they'll fuck handsome. If you're rich, they'll fuck poor. If you're poor, they'll fuck rich.

They just won't fuck you.

And these younger wives are cocky.

Well, today it ends.

Ridley's gun is waiting for him in room 216.

He finishes his coffee, rides the elevator to the second floor, enters his room. He removes the gun from its case.

Zeliska revolvers are twenty-two inches long and weigh thirteen pounds. The weight helps control the recoil.

Ridley dons his eye protectors, inserts his custom ear plugs, loads five rounds into the cylinder. He lies on his back on the bed, centers himself, and looks up at the ceiling, thinking, *my wife's twelve feet above me, fucking Tom Bell.*

He imagines Connie moaning with pleasure. Giving Tom oral. Allowing him free reign over every inch of her body.

She barely knows the guy!

Is she really capable of doing things to him she won't do for the man who loves her?

Of course she is.

That's how it works.

When they spread their legs for another man, they go all the way.

Ridley lifts his gun, extends his arms, locks them. The barrel's eight feet from Connie's back, if she's on the bottom, or Connie's front, if Tom's doing her face down. Or eight feet from Tom's back, if Connie's on top.

He cocks the gun anticipating what could happen. First, the bullet will send fragments of concrete in all directions, and cover him with concrete dust. No problem. People in the lobby might remember seeing a guy covered in dust later on, but they won't associate him with being the shooter. Second, due to freak luck, the bullet might ricochet into Ridley, and kill him instantly. That would be unlikely, but Ridley's prepared to die. If he doesn't make a clean getaway he'll be in prison the rest of his life, and he'd rather be dead than in prison. Third, the first shot might not make it all the way to the target, so he intends to pump all five rounds into the ceiling, shooting each successive shot into the hole made by the first bullet. With any luck at all, the first shot will kill whoever's on the bottom, the rest will kill whoever's on top.

Ridley takes a deep breath, lets it out slowly, then pulls the trigger.

In this enclosed area, even with his ear plugs firmly in place, the gunshot sounds like a bomb detonating. The concrete above him explodes in a cloud of smoke. Sharp pieces of plaster and concrete nick his body, and would have shredded his eyes, but for the safety goggles. The recoil nearly caused him to lose his grip. The gun gas makes him retch.

He can't see the hole his first bullet made, but makes an educated guess and fires again. This time the recoil is so fierce, Ridley's arms can't prevent the gun from shattering his face. As he cries out in pain, a two-foot slab of concrete disengages from the ceiling, hangs precariously for a split second, then falls seven feet onto Ridley's exposed neck, killing him instantly.

Chapter 1

Cincinnati, Four Days Earlier...
Donovan Creed.

"THEY'RE PLAYING MUSIC!" Callie says, with a burst of sudden enthusiasm. "You think Sal set up a dance floor?"

"I hope not," I say.

It's mid-morning, fourth of July. The sun's bright, but not yet hot. We're crossing a perfectly-manicured lawn, heading toward the main tent to greet our host, crime boss Sal Bonadello.

"Don't be a spoil sport, Donovan!"

"Spoil sport? What does that even mean?"

"It means if they play our song I expect a dance."

Here's something you don't know about me. I'm a terrible dancer. I mean, I know enough ballroom dancing to get laid. But when the music's fast and I'm dancing freestyle I look like Quasimodo trying to put on a suit.

"We don't have a song," I say.

"Are you insane? Of course we do!"

"What's ours?"

"You'll know it when you hear it."

I laugh. "So you don't know, either."

"Every couple has a song, Donovan. We just haven't heard ours yet."

"Wait. Did you just call us a couple?"

Callie sighs. "Does this make sense to you?"

"What?"

"In all these years we've never shared a dance."

"That can't be true. Perhaps you've forgotten."

"Trust me, I'd remember. I love dancing. But you avoid it like Superman avoids kryptonite."

She's right, of course. And her kryptonite analogy's a good one.

Callie and I have worked together eight years. We're assassins. She's the only person on earth I trust not to kill me, and that's only on good days. But we haven't danced because, overlooking the fact I look stupid while doing it, dance floors are high-risk locations. You're moving around, people around you are moving, you can't keep track. Is the guy in the blue suit wielding a knife? Is the older lady palming a derringer? Maybe the lady with the gun isn't on the dance floor. Maybe she's a guy dressed like an old lady, sitting at a table across the room holding a purse that contains a gun with a silencer. When she shoots, the small sound gets drowned out by the music. Maybe she's watching me dance, waiting for the perfect time to squeeze off a shot. She puts her hand in her purse, grips her gun, gives the signal. On the dance floor, a pretty redhead nods, then purposely backs into

2

me, knocks me off balance. The older lady shoots, kills me, and waltzes out the room.

Dancing's a bitch for those in our business.

But try telling that to Callie.

That said, I have great appreciation for the aesthetic beauty and athletic grace displayed by certain professional dancers with finely-honed skills.

"I love to watch highly-skilled professional dancers," I say, cheerfully.

She frowns. "Stripping doesn't count."

"Of course it does!"

"Sorry."

"Then why do they call it lap *dancing?*"

Callie shakes her head, dismissively. "You're hopeless."

I stop us in our tracks and say, "Some of the best dancers in the world are strippers. Name one person who can dance better than Gwen."

Gwen being Callie's live-in girlfriend.

"Me," she says.

I smile. "Ever thought about stripping?"

"Here's the bottom line," she says. "We're dancing today, you and me."

"*If* they have a dance floor."

Sal owns the hundred-acre field that runs behind his house. The main tent is still more than fifty yards away. As we crest a small hill we see musicians playing blue grass music.

On a stage.

We see something else.

Callie smiles, points to the dance floor.

"You'll dance with me, won't you?" she says.

"Only if my life depends on it."

"Atta boy!"

"I'll need fortification," I say.

"Of course you will."

This means Callie, frozen vodka cranberry. Me, shot of bourbon, straight up.

As we continue our journey toward the tent, people stop what they're doing to stare. Callie's wearing a raspberry floral-print cocktail dress and matching wedge sandals with bangle straps.

But that's not why they're staring.

They're staring at the work of art that is Callie Carpenter.

There are two types of people in the world: those who've seen Callie in person, and those who want to.

How pretty is she?

Astonishingly pretty. Unnaturally pretty.

Who does she *look* like?

You're joking, right?

You don't compare Callie to others. Others compare themselves to *her*.

And come up short.

I could tell you her hair's naturally blonde and her eyes piercing gray. I could tell you super models and starlets would kill to have her face *or* body, and she's got both. I could tell you her scent is better after a workout than a shower, and her breath cleaner than ionic meadow air after a lightning storm.

I could tell you all those things and more.

But nothing prepares you for seeing Callie the first time.

Unless you were a sailor in a former life whose vessel was attacked by Blackbeard the pirate.

Before attacking ships, Blackbeard used to tie dozens of strips of cloth to his beard and set them on fire. So disarming was his appearance, enemy sailors often threw their guns and swords down in terror, and dropped to their knees, making no effort to defend themselves.

Callie's looks are likewise lethal. I've seen her take down skilled assassins who were so stunned by her beauty they hesitated to pull the trigger. Their split-second pause allowed Callie just enough time to squeeze off a kill shot.

Not that it mattered. She could have easily killed these men and women with her hands, feet, or by hurling a deadly projectile, because it's not just her looks that make Callie superhuman. She's one of the most efficient killing machines on earth.

What's that? Oh. She's twenty-six.

How long?

Like I said, I've known her eight years.

What?

Ha. I wish.

Truth is, I've never even seen her naked. Never kissed her, for that matter.

I've traveled with her, dined with her, lived with her for weeks at a time.

I've killed with her.

We've saved each other's lives, shared stories, toothbrushes, even the same woman, Gwen Peters.

It's not what you think.

We didn't have a threesome. Gwen and I met first, and had sex. Then Callie met Gwen, and they had sex. Gwen moved in with Callie, and they kept having sex, but one day

Gwen and I had sex again. When Callie found out, she nearly killed Gwen, but decided to give her another chance.

I'm pretty sure Gwen and I won't be sleeping together in the foreseeable future. She appears to place a higher value on living than having sex with me.

Hard to believe, right?

So I'm out of the picture, and that's fine, since I recently discovered I've fallen in love with one of my employees.

Callie Carpenter.

No, I haven't told her. I wouldn't know how. She's completely oblivious to my feelings.

Beautiful women are clustered around us, staring at Callie. They're the girlfriends of ugly mobster men, hardened criminals who are afraid to make eye contact with me.

I make them nervous.

Why?

I'm the guy who killed their mob friends.

Frankie De Luca waves as I pass by. He's here with his wife, Angie. The De Lucas don't know it yet, but this is their last day to live. That's because Sal hired me to kill Angie tonight. Sal doesn't know it yet, but I'm going to snuff Frankie too. Sal won't approve, because Frankie's a huge earner, but Sal's my friend. He's too close to the situation to understand, but it's in his best interest for Frankie to go away too.

As we close in on the tent, two young women emerge, laughing. They glance in our direction and stop short.

We stop, too.

The four of us are twenty feet apart, staring at each other.

"She's looking at you, pretty boy," Callie murmurs.

"Which one?"

"The blonde. Recognize her?"

"Dani Ripper."

"Standing with her girlfriend, Sophie Alexander."

"Sal's niece," I say.

"Sophie's pretty," Callie says.

"Yowzer!"

"But Dani's gorgeous, don't you think?"

"Not compared to you."

"Seriously, Donovan? Because people say she could pass for my sister."

"Not your twin sister."

Callie gives me a funny look, then says, "Why are they staring at us?"

"The same reason we're staring at them."

"We're sizing each other up?"

I nod. "Think we can take 'em?"

Callie laughs, which causes Dani and Sophie to laugh.

Dani waves and hollers, "Hi, ya'll!"

"Ya'll?" I say.

Callie smiles, waves back, and whispers, "I know what I want for my birthday!"

"Dani Ripper?"

"In the flesh."

"Odd way to put it."

"That's how we talk, here in the south."

"Ah. You're a southern belle now?"

"I am if she is ... ya'll!"

We watch them turn and walk away.

And keep watching them.

"Nice ass," Callie says, under her breath.

"*Excuse me?*"

She grins like a politician at a fundraiser.

I say, "Women actually talk like that?"

"Oh please," she says. "Don't you agree? Nice ass?"

"Which one?"

"Both."

"I don't check out women's posteriors," I say. "It's rude."

She groans and rolls her eyes. "You are so full of shit!"

"Think they'll turn around?" I say.

"I guarantee it."

We watch Dani's hips sway hypnotically as she walks.

Sophie turns first, sees us staring, and laughs. She says something to Dani. A few steps later they stop and Dani sneaks a peek. They laugh again.

Callie says, "I want her, Donovan."

"Me too."

"I saw her first."

"Doesn't matter. I saw Gwen first, but she's with you."

"Tell you what," Callie says. "You can have Sophie."

"Any other day, I'd be proud to have Sophie. Though I doubt Sal would approve."

"Nothing wrong with Sophie," Callie says. "Solid eight, wouldn't you say?"

"I would."

"Dani, on the other hand ..."

"Ten."

Callie nods.

I ask, "Have you ever been with a woman as hot as Dani Ripper?"

"Not in the biblical sense. Have you?"

I wait till she turns to look at me.

We lock eyes. Then I say, "Not yet."

She smiles and looks down. Then says, "Anyway, Dani's into you, not me."

"That's crazy. She's gay."

"She only thinks she's gay. Less than a month ago she was married, remember?"

"Till her husband got killed."

"Till then," Callie says.

"Then Sophie showed up."

"Sophie got lucky."

"How so?"

"She was there to pick up the pieces when Dani was vulnerable."

"Is that how it works?" I say.

"Sometimes."

We're both quiet a moment.

"This thing between Dani and Sophie," Callie says.

"Yeah?"

She pauses, gives me a look. "It's temporary."

Chapter 2

"YOU CAME!" SAL says with great enthusiasm, as we enter the main tent.

"Sal?" I say. "Marie? This is Callie Carpenter. Callie? Sal and Marie Bonadello. Our gracious hosts."

"Thank you so much for inviting us!" Callie says.

Marie shows Callie the deepest frown her face can hold. The very response you'd expect from a seasoned wife standing face-to-face with her husband's greatest weakness.

She says, "Be forewarned, Miss Carpenter. My husband's got less class than a nut-licking dog at a church picnic."

Marie fixes her husband with a harsh gaze and leaves to greet the next guests.

Sal says, "I must apologize for my wife. She and I no longer sleep together."

Callie and I exchange WTF looks.

"Intercourse," he adds, by way of explanation. "We don't—whatcha call—"

"We get it," I say.

Callie and I press envelopes filled with cash into Sal's hand, as is the custom when attending these sorts of events. Sal separates the envelopes and hefts mine briefly.

"You've always been generous," he says. Then looks at Callie and says, "He's very—whatcha call—philanthropic."

Trying to impress her with his vocabulary.

Then he does something I've never seen him do.

He places Callie's envelope back in her hand and says, "I don't expect this from you. A goddess like you should be *paid* to attend parties!"

Callie flashes a dazzling smile. "That's so nice of you to say, Mr. Bonadello. But I insist on making a contribution to your Mothers of Sicily charity."

"They do great work," I say, sarcastically.

As he accepts her envelope a second time he says, "Please, fair maid. Call me Sal."

"Okay."

"Say it. Say my name," he says.

"Sal."

He closes his eyes and swoons.

"Didja hear that?" he says. "An angel just spoke my name."

He tucks the envelopes into his jacket pocket, then takes Callie's hand in his.

"I've invited you to my—whatcha call—*soirees* every time," he says. "But you never showed up."

She shrugs.

I notice Marie coming up behind Sal and cough to warn him. But he's too wrapped up in Callie to notice. He raises her hand to his lips and kisses it. Then takes a step back and looks her up and down like she's covered in frosting and he can't decide where to start licking.

He says, "Did you happen to bring a bikini, sweetheart?"

Marie says, "Why don't you just sniff her ass, Sal? Isn't that what dogs do?"

Chapter 3

Sophie and Dani.

SOPHIE ALEXANDER (STAGE name) is a well-known songwriter who's struggling to make it as a country singer. Her proud, supportive Uncle Sal hired her to provide the entertainment today, and flew booking agents from all over the country to watch her perform. She'd been nervous all week about it, but at the moment, she and Dani are consumed with thoughts of Callie and Creed.

"What do you think of our assassin?" Sophie says, while waiting for the sound check guy to hook up her equipment.

"He's gorgeous!"

Sophie gives her a look. "I'm talking about Callie Carpenter."

Dani laughs. "Her, too."

"She's gay, you know."

"So is he."

Sophie furrows her brow. "Who?"

13

"Donovan Creed."

Sophie laughs. "I don't think so."

"Trust me," Dani says. "When they're that beautiful and buff, they're gay."

Sophie says, "So now you're an expert?"

"Oh shit!" Dani says. "*Don't look!*"

"What's wrong?"

"They're coming over."

The prettiest woman Dani has ever seen offers her hand and says, "Hi Dani. I'm Callie Carpenter."

They shake hands. Dani says, "And you're Donovan Creed, the phony FBI agent."

Creed says, "I have no idea what you're talking about."

"Yes, you do," she says. "You somehow managed to shut down the FBI's investigation. You probably kept me out of jail."

"I probably did, but it wasn't that big a deal. I knew you didn't kill your husband."

Sophie says, "And how about you, Mr. Creed. Are you planning to kill some of our party guests today?"

Dani punches her arm. "Jesus, Sofe!"

Creed says, "I promise not to kill a single guest."

Dani notices a slight smile on Callie's lips and says, "A married one, perhaps?"

Callie changes the subject. "You enjoy being a private detective?"

"Very much. When I get to help kids."

"You're not carrying a gun."

"I own a small Glock, but hardly ever carry it."

"Because?"

14

"Guns frighten me."

Callie frowns.

Creed says, "So, you two are a couple?"

Sophie puts her arm around Dani's waist and pulls her close.

"We are," she says.

The sound guy approaches and stands a respectful distance away, waiting to be noticed.

Sophie says, "I need to do a sound check."

"I'll go with you," Callie says.

Sophie looks at Dani, standing with Creed. "Want to come?" she says.

"I'll watch from here," Dani says.

While Sophie and Callie climb the steps onto the stage, Creed leans closer to Dani and says, "What's it like?"

"What?"

"Being with a woman?"

Dani smiles, but says nothing.

After the sound check, Sophie and Callie come back over. Sophie says, "You're smiling. What did I miss?"

"I was right."

Sophie says, "You think?"

Creed says, "Right about what?"

Dani says, "You're from Vegas?"

"For the time being."

"Well, if you want, Sofe and I can show you where to find the best fashion in Cincinnati."

"Are you inviting me to go shopping with you?"

Dani looks at Sophie. Then says, "Of course! It'll be fun!"

Callie says, "Donovan, go check out the pool."

"What?"

Callie says, "Girl talk."

"Oh. Right."

Chapter 4

Donovan Creed.

SOPHIE'S SINGING, DANI'S standing left of the stage, watching her. Callie and I stand a safe distance from the crowd that's gathered to watch Sophie's band.

"Ready to dance yet?"

"Are they playing our song?"

She cocks her head and listens a moment, then wrinkles her nose.

"We need a special song," she says. "Something melodic and dreamy. Or at least something slow, with meaningful lyrics."

"I take it Love Dies doesn't cut it?"

"Not even."

"I'd like something from the sixties."

"Eighteen sixties?"

"Funny."

"This is a progressive country band," Callie says. "They're not likely to play old fogey music."

"If they do, that's our song."

"I don't plan to wait that long. The very next song they play will become our song. Say it."

"Even if it's Grandma Got Run Over by a Reindeer?"

"Even if."

"Come to think of it, that would be funny."

"Say it."

"Next song they play is our song."

"Deal," she says. "And we'll dance to it?"

"Deal," I say.

She smiles.

"You spoke to the women," I say.

"Right."

"What did you learn?"

"Dani thinks you're gay."

"*What?*"

Callie laughs.

"Why would she possibly think that?"

"She says you're too pretty to be straight. Plus, you asked what it's like to be with a woman."

"She told you I said that?"

"She did."

"Why?"

"It's part of the sisterhood code."

"I'll be right back," I say, and walk over to Dani. I have to shout for her to hear me.

"This isn't my face!" I yell.

She gives me a curious look, as if maybe the music is too loud to understand what I said. Then she hollers, "You look like that famous movie star. What's his name?"

"I don't know."

"It'll come to me," she says. "In time."

"This isn't my face," I repeat, aware that others standing nearby might be able to hear me.

She gives me that quizzical look again, and says, "Of course it's your face! Who else's face could it be?" Then she shakes her head and laughs.

"What?"

"You got me."

"What do you mean?"

"You're playing with me," she says, chuckling. "I'm a little dense sometimes. You've got a wonderful face, and I expect you know it."

"What if I used to have a huge scar, from here to here?"

She laughs. "What if *I* used to have one?"

"Did you?"

She cocks her head. "Are you always this intense?"

"Do you like intense men?"

"Honestly? They make me uncomfortable."

"Me too," I say. Then realize that probably came out wrong.

I trust Callie's gaydar. If she's right about Dani being straight, and if I can't get Callie interested in me, I intend to swarm Dani like bees on Sprite. I start to say something to position myself for such a swarm, but suddenly become aware Sophie's band has begun playing a slow, melodic sixties song with meaningful lyrics. It also happens to be, as Callie knows, one of my favorite songs.

True Love Never Runs Smooth.

Sounds fresh and nice, the way Sophie's singing it. Like maybe she learned it just for today's party?

19

Is it possible?

It is.

I can tell by the way Callie's smiling at me. The look on her face warms my heart and says it all. I take two steps toward her and my phone rings. I check the caller ID, close my eyes and groan. And accept the call.

When I hang up I notice Dani looks concerned. She approaches me.

"Are you okay?"

"I'm good. Why do you ask?"

"Your expression changed. You look upset."

"One of my best friends just died."

"Oh, you poor thing!" she says. "I'm so sorry!"

I look back to the area where Callie and I had been standing, but don't see her. I turn my head some more and squint my eyes against the sun and stare at the people entering and exiting the main tent.

Still no Callie.

Dani points to the dance floor where Callie's dancing alone.

"We'll talk later," I say, then head toward Callie.

She sees me coming and says, "You're late." Then sees my face and says, "What's wrong?"

"Lou Kelly's dead."

"What? How?"

"I'm not sure. Let's go somewhere quiet."

When we're far enough from the band to allow normal conversation I say, "I've got to meet the Homeland Security team at Sensory Resources."

"Why?"

"They claim they're offering me Darwin's job."

"Shit."

"What's wrong?"

"You'd have to move to Virginia."

"Not necessarily."

She bites the top corner of her lip. Then says, "I should come with you."

"You should. But you can't."

"Why not?"

"They might be calling me in."

"What do you mean? To kill you?"

"That's what they do, sometimes, when they're done with us."

"Then I *definitely* need to be there!"

I look down and notice she's holding my hand. She notices it too, and releases her grip.

"Sorry," she says.

I want to say something clever, but my brain won't work.

"I can't believe Lou's dead," she says.

"Me either."

"What happened?"

"They're not sure."

"What about Angie De Luca? And Frankie?"

"I'd kill them now, on the way to the car, but you know how Sal is. He'd pitch a fit."

"Not to mention he'd have a hard time getting guests to attend his next party."

I look at her. "Favor?"

"Stay here and kill the De Lucas tonight?"

I nod.

"Money?" she says.

I smile. "Fifty."

"Seems light."

"I was doing Frankie for free, remember?"

"Keep me posted," she says.

"I will."

"Regularly."

"Okay."

I wait for her to say something, but she's staring downward, thinking it through first. So I say, "What?"

"Nothing."

"Please. Say it."

She looks up at me and says, "Be careful."

I grin. "I'm always careful."

She suddenly slaps my face. Hard. Then does something that shocks the shit out of me.

She kisses my cheek.

You don't understand.

This is completely out of character for her. The kissing part, I mean.

Then she says, "Don't die on me, Donovan."

Then she adds, "Not now."

As she turns to walk away I say, "What do you mean, 'not now'?"

But she keeps walking.

Chapter 5

Callie & Dani.

"I HATE TO intrude," Dani says, moments later, "But Donovan seemed very upset over the loss of his friend. Shouldn't you be with him?"

"He's fine. And Lou Kelly wasn't much of a friend."

"I don't understand."

"Lou tried to kill Donovan. Now that he's dead, there's a vacancy in the agency that needs filling. They're offering Donovan the job. It's a huge promotion."

Dani shakes her head. "You two lead the most exciting lives."

Callie smiles. "We do. But in my case there's something missing."

"What's that?"

"The right partner."

Moments earlier, after walking away from Creed, Callie made her way to the stand of trees by the picnic area. She dragged two white wooden folding chairs twenty feet away from the tables.

"Are you and Sophie going back to Nashville tonight?"

"We're going to dinner with Sal at some restaurant where we can view the fireworks. It's supposed to be a big deal. Sophie's spending the night with Sal and Marie."

Callie arches an eyebrow. "Marie doesn't trust you in the house with Sal."

"I think it's more of a case of this all being a foreign concept to the Bonadellos."

"Your relationship with Sophie?"

Dani nods.

"So you've got to stay in a hotel by yourself."

Dani shrugs. "I don't mind. I've got plenty of work I can do."

"Please," Callie says, pointing to the empty chair. "Sit with me."

Dani looks around a moment. "I don't want to take someone's seat."

"It's for you."

"You knew I'd come?"

"I hoped you would. I moved the chairs so we could speak privately."

Dani hesitates a moment, then sits.

"You and Donovan stared at us a lot today," she says.

"That's my fault. But to be honest, I was staring at you, not Sophie."

"Why?" Dani says, showing a hint of embarrassment.

Callie pauses, then says, "I'm a woman of action. I'm better with weapons than words. I tend to be blunt in conversation."

Dani nods slowly. "I get that."

Callie says, "I'm happy to answer your question, but I don't want to offend you."

"You won't offend me."

"We'll see."

"Please," Dani says. "Tell me. I need to get back soon."

"I was staring because you're the most beautiful woman I've ever seen, and I'm incredibly attracted to you."

Dani's eyes grow larger than normal, if such could be possible. She starts to get to her feet.

"Please," Callie says. "Let me finish."

"I'm with Sophie," Dani says.

"I know. I'm not trying to seduce you."

"Forgive me, but it feels like you are. Big time."

Callie smiles. "Okay, so I am. But still. Accept the compliment."

She laughs, pats the chair.

Dani looks around again before reclaiming her seat.

"Your friend, Donovan," Dani says, changing the subject.

"What about him?"

"I'm right about him? He's gay?"

"Why do you ask?"

"Just curious."

She's not curious, Callie thinks, *she's interested.*

Callie lowers her voice and says, "This has to stay between us."

Dani nods.

"You can't tell Sophie."

"Sophie and I tell each other everything."

"Except for this,' Callie says.

25

Dani pauses, then says, "Okay."

"I'm counting on you, Dani."

Dani says nothing.

"Just to be clear," Callie says. "I can trust you, can't I?"

Dani nods several times. "Yes."

Callie looks around to make sure they're completely alone.

They are.

Callie forces herself to keep a straight face, while thinking, *Sorry Donovan. All's fair in love and war!*

Then she says, "You were right. Donovan's gay."

"I *knew* it!" Dani says, proudly.

Chapter 6

"YOU'RE *AMAZINGLY* INTUITIVE," Callie says.

"I don't know about that," Dani says.

"You might be the most intuitive person I've ever met."

"You're making fun of me."

"Not at all. You're the only one who's ever picked up on Donovan being gay."

"Seriously?"

"Except for me. I'm intuitive too."

She notices the skeptical look on Dani's face and says, "I can prove it if you like."

Dani looks around again. Callie wonders how Sophie manages to keep this gorgeous woman on such a short leash.

Dani says, "Okay, prove it. Tell me something about me no one knows."

"Can I be blunt?"

"Yes."

"I think you and Sophie are best friends."

27

Dani laughs. "Everyone knows that!"

"True. But they don't know you're not really into the sex."

Dani's smile suddenly turns upside down. "You've just crossed a line."

"Like I said, I'm a blunt person. But intuitive. I look at you and Sophie as a couple, but you know what I see?"

Dani stands. "I don't really give a shit!"

"You and Sophie aren't lovers. You've had sex once or twice, at most. I dare you to tell me I'm wrong."

Dani's eyes become slits. "You're not only blunt, you're the rudest woman I've ever met."

She stomps off, gets about twenty feet, stops. Takes a moment, then slowly walks back and sits down. Her eyes are blazing.

"What right do you have to talk to me like that?"

"I know your background," Callie says. "Sophie's taking advantage of you, and I don't like it."

"What are you *talking* about? Sofe and I love each other!"

"As friends."

"You're wrong about that."

"You're a giver. She's a taker."

"You honestly believe Sophie's using me?"

"I'm certain she is."

"You don't even *know* her!"

"I know how many times you've looked around the past five minutes to make sure she's not watching you from the stage."

"I care about Sofe. I don't want her to get the wrong impression."

"You're admitting she's jealous."

"No."

Callie smiles. "No?"

Dani says, "Fine. She's jealous. So what?"

"Do you know why people get jealous?"

She starts to speak, then stops and says, "No. I don't understand jealousy. At all."

"In every relationship there is unequal love. One partner always loves more than the other. Sophie loves you more than you love her. The less she's loved, the more jealous she gets. It's hard on her because she lives every moment knowing she could lose you."

"You don't know that."

"You agreed she's jealous. I'm telling you why. If Sophie believed you love her completely, how could she possibly get the wrong impression about us talking?"

"You're trying to fuck with my mind."

Callie fixes her with a steady stare. "I want you, Dani."

"Excuse me?"

"I want you like I've never wanted a woman in my entire life."

Dani shakes her head. "I'm sorry. I've never been around anyone like you before. I can't tell if you're fucking with me or making fun of me, or if you're just some trashy bitch who likes to stir the pot and cause trouble."

"You and I are the same, Dani."

"I seriously doubt that."

"We were both attacked by men at an early age. We both have trust issues. We're not gay, but find ourselves extremely attracted to beautiful women. We seek their nurturing. We park ourselves with women who make us feel safe, whose company we enjoy, but secretly we're looking for the right man."

"I'm sorry to hear about what happened to you. But you've known me less than an hour. You can't possibly make these types of judgments about me. Or Sophie. Nor should you say them to my face."

Callie takes her cell phone out of her handbag and says, "Answer your phone."

"It's not ringing."

Callie presses a button and says, "Yes it is."

Dani hears her cell phone ring. She frowns, clicks the button, says, "Hello?"

"It's me," Callie says.

Dani clicks to end the call and says, "How did you get *my* private number?"

"Please. The point is, now you've got my private number."

"Wow. Lucky me."

Callie says, "Look at me, Dani."

They lock eyes.

Callie says, "Tonight Sophie's going to put a lot of sexual pressure on you."

"You have no basis for saying that."

"Trust me. She saw you with Creed. She saw you with me. She'll require major reassurance."

"And what will I do?" Dani says, in a mocking tone.

"You'll try your best to prove that what you have with Sophie is the real deal. You'll think about this conversation. You'll try to prove me wrong."

Dani laughs. "You're pretty full of yourself, aren't you?"

"No. But I've been there before."

"Right. And of course, you couldn't possibly be wrong. Because you're so intuitive."

"Don't be bitchy."

"Excuse me?"

"You're not the type. Look, if I'm wrong, the worst thing that happens is you know you and Sophie are perfect together. But if I'm right, and you find yourself unable to give yourself to her completely—"

"What, I'm supposed to call you? See how a *real* woman does it?"

"Maybe you *are* the bitchy type after all," Callie says. She sighs. "Look, I'm not claiming to be a better lover than Sophie. I'm just saying you and I would have an honest relationship."

"Meaning what, exactly?"

"Our lovemaking would be based on pure lust, not obligation."

"You think I find you attractive?" Dani says.

"I know you do."

"But you're not full of yourself."

"Not in the least."

"You've got a lot of nerve!"

"And you've got the biggest, deepest, bluest eyes I've ever seen."

Dani frowns. "I will *never* make that phone call."

"Have you *never* thought about letting yourself go wild?"

"No."

"For just one night?"

"No."

31

"It'd be something we'll always have together. Something we'll never forget for the rest of our lives."

"I will never make that phone call."

"We can take it slow at first."

"You're insane."

Chapter 7

Top Six Club, Las Vegas.
Carmine Porello.

THE MOB WARS of 2008 resulted in a three-way split for control of the continental United States. The winners were Vincent "Viggie" Matisse (east coast), Sal Bonadello (mid-west), and Carmine "The Chin" Porello, who currently holds the west coast by the thinnest of threads.

Carmine's seen better days. He's late seventies, barrel-chested, with thin arms and wispy gray hair he combs straight back and holds in place with some type of ancient hair tonic. He got his nickname because twenty years ago he could lift his chin and cause the death of any ten men. These days he spends his days negotiating blow jobs from the strippers at his dance club, the *Top Six*.

"New girl's here, Mr. Porello," Roy says.

"What's she look like?"

"A headliner."

Carmine looks up with sudden interest. "Top shelf?"

"Don't get too excited. She's no Gwen Peters."

"Her and everyone else on the planet," Carmine says.

He goes quiet a minute, lost in thoughts about little Gwennie, who put the Top Six on the map and kept it there till she ran off and married Lucky Peters, the famous gambler. Gwen wasn't just beautiful, she was brilliant when it came to strip club entertainment. She invented drinking games and audience participation games that revolutionized the industry and increased business tenfold. Other clubs mimicked her style, stole her ideas, but none could compete. It was Gwen, with her looks, her personality, who brought magic to the place.

That was a year ago, and it's been all downhill ever since.

For the Top Six and all the other clubs.

After Lucky died, Carmine and his competitors tried to hire Gwen to resurrect their businesses. But she found a Vegas billionaire who keeps her happy as a pampered, kept woman. With Gwen out of the picture the club owners have been falling all over themselves in an effort to hire a headliner who could turn out to be the next Gwen Peters. But it's like catching lightning in a bottle. In Vegas pretty girls are a dime a dozen. But most of them don't have to strip for a living. Those who hang around do so because they can't score a better job elsewhere.

Carmine sighs. "They're all less than Gwen."

"True."

"How much less is this one?"

Roy shrugs. "I give her body a high eight."

"Maybe a nine?"

"Maybe."

"You saw her tits?"

Roy nods.

"They real?" Carmine says.

"Real and nice," he says. "Real nice."

Carmine says, "P, N, or Q?" Referring to a stripper game Gwen invented where clients try to guess if a penny, nickel, or quarter is sufficient to cover the areola.

"Nickle."

Carmine licks his lips. "Nickle's my favorite."

Roy, thinking, *No shit. I've only heard that what, eight thousand times?*

"How old is she?" Carmine says.

"Eighteen."

"You check her driver's license?"

"Yeah," Roy says, thinking, *After all this time you need to ask me that? I'd love to shove my fist up your dinosaur ass and grind your knuckle bones into dice, you disgusting old letch!*

"How's her face?" Carmine says.

"A nine."

"A high nine?"

"No. But a solid nine."

"Can she dance?"

"Who knows? She'll only audition for you."

"And you put up with that?"

Roy shrugs. "Like I say, she's a headliner. An eight body, a nine face. A solid eighty-nine. With a ten smile. We need her. She knows it."

Carmine Porello laughs. "Spunky. I like that. Send her in."

Roy stands, walks to the door, opens it. Says, "Mr. Porello will see you now."

The young, well-proportioned blonde who enters the office does so with an air of great confidence. She takes the seat directly across from Carmine's desk and waits for him to speak.

"You're not that cute," Carmine says.

"Yes I am."

"I've seen cuter."

"Me too. But not in this club."

"You got a mouth on you," Carmine says.

"I'm just saying what I know, Mr. Porello. If you've got prettier girls than what I've seen, you should let this bunch go."

He looks at Roy, says, "You believe this shit?"

Roy says, "Show some respect."

To Carmine, she says, "What happened to his hand?"

Carmine looks at Roy, then back at her. "He broke it."

"That's too much cast for a broken hand."

"Let's move along with the interview," Carmine says, softening his tone. "What's your name, sugar?"

"My driver's license says Willow."

He laughs. "Willow what?"

"Breeland."

"You're young."

She says nothing.

"Ever dance before?"

She nods.

"Where?"

"I'd rather not say."

"If you're gonna work for me, there won't be any secrets between us."

"Does that mean you'll tell me everything I want to know about *your* business?"

Carmine and Roy do a double-take.

Carmine says, "You believe this shit?"

Roy says, "Show some respect. I won't tell you again."

Willow says, "Where I come from, respect is a two-way street."

Carmine says, "Where *do* you come from?"

"Midwest."

"Fresh off the bus?"

"Airline. I've got a *bank account*."

"Oh, a bank account!" Roy says. "Wow!"

Willow frowns.

Carmine says, "You got references?"

"All the references I need are under my clothes."

Carmine swallows his urge to slap her face. This fuckin' eighteen-year-old comes waltzing in here like she owns the place. Cocky, arrogant, showing no respect. She sure as shit ain't no Gwen Peters. Gwen may have been confident, but she wasn't cocky. She knew her place in the hierarchy. That said, Carmine finds himself drawn to this mouthy little Willow. He wants to see her dance. Wants to see what's under her clothes. It's just that she needs to be brought down a peg.

"Let's see what you got," he says.

Willow lifts her tank top.

Carmine forces himself not to lick his lips or drool. But the fact is Willow's tits are perfect. He strains to contain his enthusiasm. Forces himself to say, "Not bad."

37

Then he adds, "Roy says you've got a great smile."

"Roy's right."

"Show me."

Willow flashes her money smile.

"I'd like to see that smile wrapped around my dick," Carmine says, attempting to put her in her place.

Roy laughs.

Without batting an eye, Willow says, "If we're negotiating, let's leave Roy out of it from here on."

Roy moves toward her with his fist cocked. But Carmine waves him off.

Roy says, "Say the word, I'll beat that attitude out of her."

Carmine says, "Leave us be, Roy. Can't you see we're negotiating?"

Willow smiles.

Roy glares at her. Says, "This ain't over, bitch."

Willow says, "Run along, Roy."

"What the *fuck* did you just say to me?"

He gets right up in her face. His eyes are slits. His face, a mask of fury. Through clenched teeth he says, "Get ready, Miss. Because I've got *plans* for *you!*"

"Cancel them," she says.

"Outside this club, you're on *my* turf," he snarls. "Bad things happen on my turf. You been warned."

Willow gives him a look of her own. Then says, "Roy, you're a bug on my windshield. Nothing more."

When he leaves, Carmine says, "You got balls, I'll give you that. But you better re-think this thing with Roy."

"Why's that?"

"He's a mean son of a bitch."

Willow shrugs.

"I won't lie to you. He beats the shit out of the girls sometimes."

Willow yawns.

"I'm serious. He broke a girl's jaw once, for talking back. Crushed another one's cheekbones."

Willow says, "I'm not afraid."

"Why not?"

She bats her goldenrod eyes at him and says, "You'll take care of me."

Carmine gives her a long look, then says, "The other girls think Roy's the power around here."

"Why should you and I care what they think?"

Carmine scrunches up his face in thought and says, "Roy thinks I'm ripe for the plucking."

"What's that mean?"

"He's one step away from making a run at me."

"Then maybe we should put him in his place."

Carmine gives her a long, wistful look.

His voice softens. "You remind me of things from long ago."

"What sorts of things?"

"Honey-suckle. Swimming at Blue Lake. Stick ball. Kick the can. You know, kid things."

He smiles.

Willow says, "Who's the first girl you ever felt up?"

"Excuse me? Did you just say 'felt up'?"

She nods.

"You mean kissed?"

"Nope. Felt up."

He laughs. "Seriously?"

"I'm told you never forget your first feel."

"Mary Jane Milligan."

She smiles. "How old were you?"

"Fourteen."

"And she was?"

"The same. During lunch she'd stand by the oak tree in the school yard, let you feel her up for a quarter."

Willow laughs. "A quarter?"

"Don't laugh. That was a big number in those days."

"Did she lift up her shirt, or what?"

"In the early days she'd flash you for a quarter. But the boys grew wise to it."

"What do you mean?"

"They'd keep an eye on her. When she got a customer they'd run over and surround her and try to catch a free peek."

"So she modified her business plan? From flashing to fondling?"

Carmine throws his head back and laughs. "Modified her business plan!" he says. He laughs some more.

Then says, "What, you attended Harvard Business School?"

"I wish."

He laughs again, and dabs the corners of his rheumy eyes with his sleeve.

"Milligan," Willow says. "Irish, yes?"

He nods.

"Catholic girl? Red hair?"

"You're good, I'll give you that!"

"Freckles?"

He nods again.

"Big boobs?"

He throws back his head and roars with laughter.

"What?"

"She was only fourteen!"

"So? Big boobs, or no?"

He laughs. "My *father* had bigger tits. But Mary Jane was the only game in town."

"Did she let you touch them, or just her blouse?"

Carmine shakes his head and chuckles. "You really want to hear this?"

"Who wouldn't?"

"I've known you five minutes, I'm tellin' you shit my wife don't know after fifty-five years of marriage."

"You're going to tell me lots of things your wife doesn't know."

"You think so, huh?"

Willow smiles.

"I never met anyone like you before," he says.

"I know," Willow says. "And you never will."

Chapter 8

Washington, D.C.
Donovan Creed.

I WORK FOR Sensory Resources, a clandestine branch of Homeland Security, headquartered eighty-five miles south-west of Bedford, Virginia, on two hundred acres of government land. My job is to recruit, train, and supervise assassins to help me kill suspected terrorists on American soil.

How do we determine the death-worthiness of a group or individual?

Good question.

Because there's no one-size-fits-all among terrorists, and no handbooks, and because information is often spotty, we follow the advice of the celebrated early-American folk hero, frontiersman, soldier, and statesman, Davy Crockett, who said, "Be sure you're right, and then go ahead," which for us roughly translates into "Kill first, ask questions later."

Because the government doesn't recognize us, they can't pay us. But we're resourceful. We steal from our victims. Perform free-lance hits for the mob. Use insider information to enhance the return on our investment portfolios.

The importance of today's meeting is underscored by my private jet's receipt of clearance to land on the Sensory Resources airstrip, which is normally reserved for the two fighter jets we keep on twenty-four-hour alert. Though I've been with the agency more than a dozen years, this is only the fourth time I've touched down on the home-field runway.

Let me catch you up to speed. The former head of Sensory was a guy named Darwin, whom everyone thinks was killed by my one-time facilitator, Lou Kelly. Lou was all set to take Darwin's place, but he turned up dead.

Here's the twist: everyone thinks Darwin was the code name for my friend, Doc Howard, but the real Darwin is alive and well. His name is Dr. Eamon Petrovsky. He's a retired surgeon living in Vegas.

I call him Dr. P.

Dr. P. will soon be heading up Vegas Moon, the plastic surgery center and spa I plan to open as a sideline business in a few weeks.

With Lou Kelly suddenly dead, panic has set in among the six people on earth who possess detailed knowledge of our little group of government assassins. Those six are currently sitting on the other side of the door I'm staring at, in the agency's conference room. Their meeting started at ten this morning. Shortly thereafter they called me, told me to come immediately. Charter a private jet. Land on site.

I get that. Time is of the essence. Decisions need to be made.

But in typical government fashion, they've got me sitting on my hands in the ante room while doctors, scientists, and members of Sensory's elite security staff enter and exit the room practically nonstop.

After two hours of sitting, I tell the young guard if they want me they can find me in my office down the hall.

"My orders are to keep you here in the ante room, sir," the guard says, nervously.

"Why?"

"To protect you."

I laugh.

He laughs.

I say, "I'll be in my office, son."

He looks uncomfortable.

"I've got bourbon there," I say, then add, "You can join me, Tommy, if you like."

He bites his lip.

This is a nice kid, Tommy Cooper. I knew his dad. I'm the one who got Tommy this guard job at Sensory. Though he's young, he's a stone killer, an elite fighting man.

I see the fingers of his right hand twitch ever-so-slightly.

"Tommy," I say.

"I take my job seriously, Mr. Creed."

I sigh. "I know you do, son."

"Then please, sir. Stay in the room with me."

"I've been here two hours."

"Yes sir."

"It's Pappy Van Winkle bourbon, Tommy."

"I get off duty at midnight," he says. "In case that offer's still on the table."

I like this kid. He reminds me of me, except for the part about following orders.

I look at my watch.

"Tommy, out of respect for your father, I'll give them two more hours. Then I'm drinking."

"Thank you, sir."

"You understand what I'm saying, son?"

"Yes sir."

"Tell me."

"You're giving me two hours to live."

"That's what I'm saying."

Chapter 9

AN HOUR LATER the conference room door opens and everyone walks out.

"Bathroom break," Sherm Phillips says, as he walks past me.

Sherm's failure to shake my hand wasn't a slight. He knows I don't shake hands. In my line of work I have to assume any attempt to touch me is an attempt on my life. The other members of the Homeland Security team know that, too. They won't even make eye contact with me.

The Sherm Phillips here is the same one you know as the U.S. Secretary of Defense. When he returns from the bathroom he says, "Sorry for the wait. Give us five more minutes, okay?"

"Okay."

Sherm's a good guy. One of the few I've met in government who actually thinks our country is more important than his job title.

Twenty minutes later the door opens and I'm invited to join them.

"Good luck, sir," Tommy says as I pass in front of him.

I stop a moment and look him in the eyes.

"Am I being set up?" I say.

"I don't know, sir."

I search his face for deception, but find none.

"Don't do it, son."

"We're on the same side, Mr. Creed."

"They always say that. Until we're not."

"Understood."

I continue into the conference room where the Big Six are seated around the polished oak table. Sherm's there, as is Randolph Scott, Director, Homeland Security. Senator Colin Scherer gives me a nod. Annie Lorber and Emerson Watkins virtually ignore me. They're the children of Sensory's co-founders, Bill Lorber and Bob Watkins, both deceased. The sixth member is chairing the meeting.

"Mr. Creed," he says, "I'm Preston Mooney, agency director, LSR. I think you know the others. Please, take a seat."

The table seats twelve. Mooney's at the head, with the others flanking him, which means there are six empty seats between us. I sit at the foot of the table, keeping as many seats between us as possible. At the same time, I realize my back is to the door.

I don't like having my back to the door, and it probably shows because Mooney says, "You seem tightly wound, Mr. Creed."

"If you've summoned me here to kill me, you've made a big mistake."

"I don't understand," he says.

"We're in the same room," I say.

I remove three quarters from my pocket, stand, walk to the door, and push them into the door jamb, effectively locking us all in the room together.

"Donovan," Sherm says. "Relax. No one's trying to kill you."

"I want to believe you," I say, "but my senses are on high alert."

"What's that supposed to mean?" Mooney says.

Sherm says, "It means if someone suddenly farts, none of us will live to smell it."

Annie Lorber wrinkles her nose in disgust.

I reclaim my seat.

"What's LSR?" I say. "What do you do?"

"That information is beyond your pay grade," Mooney says.

"You don't pay me."

"Excuse me?"

"I don't get paid for my work, here. I have to moonlight to pay the bills."

"What are you *talking* about?"

"You said your agency's initials are beyond my pay grade. I don't have a pay grade."

Preston Mooney rolls his eyes. "It's a figure of speech," he says.

"I don't really care about the initials," I say. "But I *do* want to know what happened to Lou Kelly."

Mooney gives me a sour look.

"I'm told you're a primitive man," he says. "But be advised there are parliamentary rules and procedures for conducting a meeting. As long as I'm chairman, we'll follow those rules."

I look at Sherm Phillips, who shakes his head as if to say, "See what I have to deal with every day?"

Chapter 10

"AS THE OTHER members of the committee are aware," Mooney says, "Lou Kelly accidentally contracted dimethylmercury poisoning."

"Accidentally?" I say.

Sherm Phillips says, "Miles Gundy's work."

I nod. Miles Gundy, now deceased, was a disgruntled corporate chemist-turned-urban terrorist.

Sherm adds, "The poison was spread by physical contact. Apparently Gundy combined it with a five hour virus."

"What about Lou's girlfriend?"

"Sherry Cherry?"

I nod.

"Dead."

Sherry was Rachel Case's mother. Rachel being my former girlfriend. Current girlfriend, if you're asking her. Rachel's being held in an underground bunker in the government facility at Mt. Weather where government scientists are harvesting her eggs.

But that's another story for another time.

"Do you have a final body count?" I ask Sherm.

Sherm's answer is interrupted by a banging sound. All eyes turn to Preston Mooney, who has a little circular cylinder of wood on the table that he's hitting with—I shit you not—a miniature wooden gavel.

"*Order!*" he shouts.

"Seriously?" I say.

"Gundy's total body count was eight hundred sixty," Sherm says.

Mooney gives him a withering look.

"Sorry," Sherm says.

Mooney clears his throat. "The reason we sent for you—"

"I'll take the job," I say.

"Excuse me?" Mooney frowns. "You can't just come in here and—"

"Can someone *else* in here do the job?" I say.

They look around the table at each other. The short answer is no.

"Does someone here *want* the job?" I say.

They search each other's faces again.

I say, "Do you have any outside candidates in mind?"

Mooney says, "There are a number of gifted people we can transition into the job."

"Seriously?"

He smiles a thin-lipped smile. "Does that surprise you, Mr. Creed?"

"Yes. And delights me, as well."

He frowns. "How so?"

"I can't tell you how many things I'd rather do than be head of Sensory Resources."

I stand, preparing to leave.

"Wait. Sit down," Mooney says. "We haven't begun the questioning!"

"With all due respect, I have no interest in being Director of Sensory Resources."

"None?"

"None."

"Why?"

"It's a shit job."

Mooney says, "You were informed by phone you were a candidate?"

"I was."

"But you aren't interested in the job?"

"That's correct."

Mooney looks around the table. "Who else has a prospective candidate?"

Emerson Watkins and Annie Lorber look at each other, but say nothing. I wonder what that's about.

Mooney looks at me. "If you don't want the job, why did you say you'd take it?"

"I thought you needed me."

They look at each other. Some are indignant, others puzzled.

Annie Lorber says, "Why would you volunteer to do a job you hate?"

"To protect my country."

Director Scott says, "Good answer. You've got the job."

Mooney says, "He needs to be interviewed first. There are procedures."

Senator Scherer says, "Fuck the procedures. He's got us by the balls."

Director Scott says, "There are no other candidates, Preston. You know it, I know it, he knows it."

Mooney says, "The committee has spent a great deal of time and effort preparing a list of questions to determine the candidate's suitability for the job!"

Sherm says, "Those are *your* questions, Mr. Chairman, not ours."

Mooney bangs the gavel and raises his voice. "I'm the government liaison to Sensory Resources. I report directly to the President! I *will* be heard!"

Sherm says, "Creed already answered the only two questions that count. He hates the job and loves his country. Anything else you ask is as helpful as whale shit on a hockey rink."

Mooney says, "These questions need to be asked. It's part of the process. His responses will be sealed in his permanent file."

"Maybe you can just look up all the shit I did in elementary school," I say, trying to be helpful. "The principal assured me it would all go on my permanent record."

"Question number one," Mooney says, looking at his notes. "Which political party do you endorse?"

"Neither," I say.

"No one's neutral. You either lean one way or the other."

"I kill Democrats and Republicans alike. And anyone else who needs killing. And yes, that includes religious persuasions, in case that's your next question."

Mooney frowns and reads from his sheet. "Question number two. What is your religious preference?"

His face turns red.

He scans three pages of questions and finally comes up with this:

"Have you ever killed a man?"

The committee members look at each other, then at me, then burst out laughing.

"What's so funny?" Mooney says.

"You want me to ask him a *real* qualifying question?" Sherm says. "Suppose a dozen secret service personnel are jogging with the President, and we get a rumor one plans to kill him. What do you do?"

"Kill them all."

Mooney blurts out, "What is this, a joke? The secret service is the most highly-trained security force on earth!"

"They're easy targets," I say.

"Why?"

"Their job is to protect the President."

"So?"

"Who's protecting them?"

"You're hired!" Director Scott shouts.

Mooney says, "Wait. You'd kill innocent, loyal security personnel based on a rumor?"

"Who wouldn't?"

Mooney's face looks like he tasted shit pie and didn't care for it.

"I have two quick questions, if you don't mind," Annie Lorber says.

I look at her.

She says, "Have you ever heard the name Tara Siegel?"

"Yes."

"And did she kill my father?"

"Yes."

"Why?"

"That's three questions."

"I beg your pardon?"

"You said two quick questions. I answered them. Now you've asked a third."

"I'll ask all the fucking questions I want!"

"Thank you, Miss Lorber."

"And you will answer them, if—"

She stops herself.

I smile.

"If I want this job?"

Chapter 11

ANNIE LORBER'S SMOLDERING eyes and angry expression tell me all I need to know about the support I can expect from her. And the way Emerson's patting her wrist to calm her down tells me their relationship has progressed beyond the boardroom. So that's two who'd say yes to killing me, should it come to a vote.

The others are harder to read.

Emerson speaks up.

"Mr. Creed, Annie's father and mine were murdered years ago. You just informed us Tara Siegel was involved."

To the committee he says, "Have any of you heard the name Tara Siegel?"

It appears not.

Emerson continues. "Tara was the Donovan Creed of the east coast at one time, meaning she worked for Sensory in that area. It's easy to piece together what happened. She wanted to take over the program back then, the same way Lou

Kelly wanted to take over recently: by killing the top people. My point is this: No one in this room has heard of Tara Siegel, and Annie and I only heard of her very recently. And she's been dead for years. Killed, apparently, by another of our Sensory operatives."

I try to maintain a poker face in all business encounters, but that comment nearly raises my eyebrows. Because other than me, only five people in the world are supposed to know who killed Tara Siegel.

And two of them are dead.

"So?" I say.

"And none of us knew who Darwin was until Lou killed him."

"So?"

"I think this proves we need more transparency in the agency. We've got trained killers running around all over the country. We're responsible for the actions of this agency, but don't have the slightest idea who's working for us."

"That's the nature of the committee, Emerson," Sherm says. "If we knew their names, we'd be targets. Our families ... would be targets."

"I've heard that all my life. But I don't understand it."

Sherm starts to say something, but I wave it off, saying, "Allow me."

I look at Emerson and say, "Transparency's a two-way street. If you know that John Smith is working for us, killing terrorists, John Smith will know who you are, and where you live. And if he gets caught and tortured, you can bet he'll give up your names and addresses. The terrorists would gladly target your families, relatives, and friends. And of course, they'd kill you as well."

"You have all this information about us," Annie says. "What keeps you from giving us up to a skilled torturer?"

Sherm says, "You read the report."

Annie frowns. "What do you mean?"

"Donovan enjoys it."

"Enjoys what?"

"Being tortured."

"You're saying our family's lives are dependent on this man's ability to withstand torture?"

"Not just our families," Sherm says. "The whole country."

"That's a bit hyperbolic, don't you think?" she says.

"Again, Annie, you've read the reports. Darwin's operatives have prevented more than twenty catastrophic events from occurring, any one of which would have crippled our capacity to function normally. And Creed recently killed more than fifty terrorists around the world with the single press of a button."

"Your point?"

"My point is, this agency works. It has protected our society, our way of life, for many years. I'm sorry about your fathers. I'm sorry about Darwin and Lou Kelly. But Creed's been with us from the inception. He's had access to all our personal information for all these years, and no one's been hurt as a result."

Mooney bangs his gavel again, seeking attention.

"This is the most ridiculous conversation I've ever heard. You're trusting America's security to a psychotic killer who enjoys being tortured. And giving him full reign over a team of computer geniuses and psychotic killers whose names we're not allowed to know."

Sherm shrugs.

Preston says, "I want it on record I strongly oppose Donovan Creed's appointment. I consider him unstable, unethical, and a serious threat to society."

Everyone goes quiet until I ask, "What does that mean?"

"It means you've got the job," Director Scott says.

"I thought I had to be approved unanimously."

"You were."

"When?"

"Just now."

"What about Mr. Mooney? Everything he just said?"

"That's him covering his ass. Isn't that right, Preston?"

"I'm done with this," Mooney says.

"Thanks for your vote, Preston," I say.

"Don't speak to me, Creed. You don't exist in my world."

"Thank you, Mr. Mooney."

An hour later I'm sitting at my desk at Sensory Resources, when my cell phone buzzes.

It's Preston Mooney.

"How'd I do?" he says.

"Perfect. You even had *me* convinced you're a toad."

"You think they bought it?"

"That we're enemies? Absolutely! They'll want your blessing before trying to kill me."

"Which means I can warn you," he says.

"Unless you're in on it."

"Surely you trust *me!*"

"I trust no one."

He sighs. "So you say."

"Give my regards to the President."

"Will do."

I hang up and call Callie.

"What's the good word?" she says.

"I took the job."

"Shit. Now I'll never see you."

"Lucky you," I say.

She says nothing.

I say, "How's it going on your end?"

"It'll be dark soon. I'm good to go."

I want to tell her how I feel.

"Callie?"

"Yeah?"

I pause. How do I put into words I love her, without having her laugh in my face?

She's waiting for me to say something.

I chicken out.

"Let me know when you're done," I say.

"I always do."

She pauses.

"Donovan?"

"Yeah?"

She pauses some more. Then says, "Is everything okay?"

"Everything's fine."

"Okay then," she says, and hangs up.

My security monitor beeps. I glance at it and see the young guard, Tommy Cooper standing outside my office door. I press the audio button.

"You're early for that drink, son," I say. "Are you coming to kill me after all?"

"No sir. I'm here to escort you to Geek City."

Chapter 12

YOU CAN'T ENTER my office without my knowledge because every office, every wing of Sensory, operates under the highest possible security conditions. Access to my area requires a retinal scan by either me or Lou Kelly, followed by the entry of a personal key code. Since Lou is no longer with us, there are only three methods of entry. One, if I'm with you. Two, if I'm in my office and click the door open. And three, you can demolish a portion of the two-foot thick concrete and steel-reinforced walls.

Because of my position in the company, and tenure, I've gained larger chunks of access over the years. But the two areas I have never been permitted access are Lou's office and Geek City.

Geek City is the area that houses Lou's Geek Squad, the world's foremost group of computer experts and researchers. It took years for Lou to assemble and train this team, and he's the only person they've ever worked for at Sensory. These geeks are so valuable they're the sole reason I allowed Lou to live after he attempted to kill me.

Why didn't I just kill Lou and run the team myself?

They're loyalty is to Lou. Had I killed him, they'd have turned on me. But because I spared Lou's life, I'm hoping we can find a common ground. I can't do this job without the geeks.

I've never met them. For years I've pestered Lou about his geeks, but all I've managed to glean in all that time is they are five in number, they haven't left the confines of Geek City for more than ten years, and they're eunuchs.

That's right, eunuchs.

I press the button on my desk that unlocks my office door. Cooper enters.

"Ready, sir?"

"Have a seat, Tommy," I say.

He looks around. "Where, sir?"

There are no chairs in my office. I don't meet people here. Callie has seen my office, as has Miranda, my favorite hooker, but both were walk-throughs. I did happen to catch Lou Kelly fucking Sherry Cherry on my desk not long ago, but Lou assured me that was a one-time deal. Had Tommy not looked around for a chair just now, I'd wonder if *he'd* been in here before.

I stand, grab my laptop, and we start walking.

"Has anyone spoken to the geeks since Lou died?"

"Not to my knowledge, sir."

"What about the people who bring them food?"

"Their supplies are placed on a conveyor. No one sees the geeks."

"Have you thought of starving them out?"

"No sir."

"Seems to me you could stop putting food on the conveyor, force them to come out."

"Apparently they've squirreled away enough canned goods and bottled water to survive for many months. But that's not the issue, sir," Tommy says.

"What's the issue?"

"Until you got the job today, no one was authorized to talk to the geeks, nor did anyone have any interest in doing so."

"Do you know their names?"

"No, sir."

"Aren't you curious about them?"

"Not at all."

He stops us a moment and says, "May I be frank, sir?"

"Please do."

"I'm not one to spread rumors. But from what I've heard, the less contact I have with them the better."

"What's the rumor, son?"

"I've heard Geek City's a leper colony."

I laugh.

He frowns. "They're not lepers?"

"I can't say for sure. But wouldn't lepers have trouble typing on keyboards?"

"I don't know."

"They're not lepers, son. They're choirboys."

"Choirboys, sir?"

"That's all I'm going to say about it."

"Yes, sir."

Chapter 13

TOMMY ESCORTS ME to the outer chamber of Geek City, which means the beeper has sounded within their compound. By now they're staring at us through their monitors.

But nothing happens.

"Hi, guys," I say. "I'm Donovan Creed."

No answer.

Then I realize what's going on.

"Tommy," I say, "Please leave me here."

"It could be dangerous."

"Look at me, son."

He does.

"I'm Donovan Creed."

"Yes sir."

He pauses, then says, "Please program my number in your phone, sir, just to be safe."

He gives me his number and leaves.

Moments later the door clicks open.

Chapter 14

THE FIRST THING you'll notice upon entering the lobby of Geek City is the noise.

It's deafening.

Like a thousand live bands playing at the same time. All styles. Some of the songs sound like they're being played backwards. Others, sideways.

Each song is being played at ear-piercing decibels. When they come together, it's complete chaos. Agony for the ears. I make a mental note to explore the use of this taped music as a crowd-control weapon.

The lobby is small, with a redwood picnic-style table and two benches on one side, a couch and coffee table on the other. I take a seat at the picnic table for two reasons. One, I may have to jump to my feet quickly, to defend myself, and two, I don't know these people. The couch could be a germ pit.

I'm alone in the lobby, but I know they're watching. While I see no cameras, I *feel* them studying me.

"Can someone please turn down the music?" I shout.

The music mutes.

A moment later a door opens, and three people enter the lobby in lock-step. They include a midget, a dwarf, and what appears to be an elf.

"I'm Curly," the first one says. "I've always preferred Kathleen to your other lady friends, but hey, what do I know? I'm a eunuch, right? It's your love life to screw up, and my job to chronicle your screw ups. Still, I never understood your fascination with Rachel. You know she plans to kill you, right?"

"I'm Larry," the second one says. "I'm a fan of Callie. I think you've got a window of opportunity there, but it won't be easy getting her away from Gwen."

"You must be Moe," I say to the third.

The three put their hands over their hearts and look down, solemnly.

"Something wrong?" I ask.

"Moe hung himself when Lou died," the third one says. "You can call me C.H."

"What does that stand for?"

"It's the first two letters of my name. I go by C.H. because you'd never be able to pronounce my name properly."

"It's that difficult, is it?"

"You can't imagine."

"I've got a pretty good ear for names."

"It's a secret name," he says. "Very few people know it."

I stare at him a moment. "C.H. it is," I say. Then add, "I'm sorry to hear about Moe. I'm sure he'll be missed. Where's the other one?"

They look at each other, confused.

"Lou told me there were five of you."

They put their hands over their hearts and look down at their feet again.

And start to cry.

"What now?" I say.

"Lou was the fifth," Larry says.

"Oh. Sorry."

Curly says, "Now it's you. But you don't research. At all. Nor do you compute."

"But he adventures!" C.H. says, brightly. "And when he does, we do!"

C.H. is the elfin one. If I knew him better, and could kid around, I'd ask him where he's from, the forest or meadows? But I don't want to offend him. I mean, I know there's no such thing as elves.

Although I look at him and have to wonder.

"Guys," I say, "I'm not Lou Kelly, and could never replace him in a million years. But I've always respected your work. Thanks to you, we managed to stop Miles Gundy from killing more kids."

"Don't be modest, Mr. Creed," C.H. says. "You and Miranda gave us the proper search parameters. And you did all the killing. I'm happy to welcome you to the team. Especially since learning Miranda will be working with us. She's my personal favorite. Do you think I might be able to meet her someday?"

"Are you saying you'll work with me?"

"Only you," he says. Then he shouts, "The Platters! Nineteen-fifty-five!"

Larry shouts, "Mercury Records. But it was their *second* release! Don't forget that!"

Curly says, "Buck Ram wrote it for the Ink Spots."

They make a little huddle, put their hands low and shout, "Heyyyy!" as they raise them up over their heads.

Each of them has a favorite joke, and I'm asked to listen and pick a favorite. The jokes are so poorly conceived and delivered, I chuckle throughout the telling to cover the fact I can't decipher the punch lines.

"They're equally funny," I say, shamelessly.

"Not good enough," Curly says. "You have to choose a favorite."

I frown. It'd be easier to view Hell's menu and choose between the unwashed tripe, fermented squid guts, and pig organs wrapped in flesh.

I pick one of the jokes and make two of my new friends unhappy.

But get the sense we're bonding.

"Do you have an assignment for us?" Curly says.

I place my laptop on the redwood picnic table.

"I don't speak computer, so this won't sound professional."

"Go ahead."

"I want you to configure my computer in such a way that we can communicate in code. You send me a coded message, I respond in code. But since I don't have the time or desire to learn a code, I want to type a password that turns your code into plain English so I can read it. When I type a response, I add a different password to the message and it changes my English back to your code. But my responses would also work with the first code."

They look at each other a moment, stunned, then burst into laughter. Finally Larry says, "Yeah, we can do that." Then he repeats what I said and they fall on the floor laughing hysterically, roll around, grabbing their sides.

"Plain English!" Curly yells between peals of laughter.

"Coded message!" Larry says, shaking with delight.

When at last they calm down, C.H. says, "Why a different code for the response?"

"If someone captures me and forces me to send you a message, I'll use the same code both times. That way you'll know something's wrong."

All three nod, sagely.

"I also want you to put a tracer on the computer, so you'll know where I am at all times."

They look at each other again, but refrain from laughing.

"That requires a lot of trust on your part," C.H. says.

"I do trust you guys," I say.

"That's good," Curly says. "Because we've been tracing your laptop since the day you got it."

Larry says, "There's a bomb in there, too."

"Excuse me?"

"There's a bomb in your laptop. All we have to do is go online, punch in a code, and your computer blows up."

"I got my laptop directly from the factory."

"Yes. But you ordered it online from your old computer."

"So?"

"We have a keystroke capture system on all your devices. Everything you type, every message you receive, comes to us. We read your computer order, hacked into the company's system, had your new laptop routed to our address, assembled the tracking device, key capture, and bomb, and shipped it on to you."

"How powerful a bomb is it?"

"Not that powerful," C.H. says. "It has a blast area of four to ten feet, depending on if your laptop is open or not."

I look at my laptop.

"There's a bomb inside?"

"Yes."

"If I'm carrying it, and you press the code, I could die?"

"Yes, of course."

Curly says, "It's not that big a deal. There's a bomb in all the computers."

"What are you saying?"

"You, Jarvis, Maybe, Gwen, Joe Penny, Jeff Tuck—"

"What about Callie?" I ask.

"We can't get access to anything owned by Callie."

"Why not?"

"She's too careful."

"More careful than me?"

They all start laughing again.

I say, "You're telling me you could kill me and all my crew with the simple entry of a code?"

"Yes, provided you're near your computers."

"You could wait for us to start typing, then kill us."

Curly turns to Larry and says, "By George, I think he's got it!"

I say, "Who authorized you to plant bombs in our computers?"

"Darwin."

"Wait. Which Darwin?"

"As you well know, there's only one Darwin. Dr. Petrovsky."

"You knew who Darwin was all this time and never told anyone?"

"Yes."

"Why not?"

"No one ever asked us."

"But Lou thought Dr. Howard was Darwin. He killed him."

C.H. shakes his head as if saddened by my intellectual inefficiency. He says, "Dr. Petrovsky paid Lou forty million dollars to kill Dr. Howard and frame him for being Darwin. It was part of his exit plan."

"Does Dr. P. still possess the code?"

"Yes. Should we change it?"

I do a double take. Dr. P., my new business partner, could have killed me and the entire crew, all but Callie, at any time. And still can.

"Don't change the code. Cancel it. Immediately."

Larry salutes me. "Yes, sir!"

"What about your agents?" C.H. says.

"Theirs, too."

"But what if you want to kill them sometime?" Larry asks.

"I don't kill my friends," I say.

They look at each other.

"What?"

C.H. says, "Why does the name Augustus Quinn come to mind?"

I frown. "That's different."

He says, "It's always different when *they* do it."

"Can you disable the kill code while I wait?"

"Of course."

Larry says, "I assume you'll want us to clear you for a retinal scan."

I say, "No. This is your home. I know how much you value your privacy."

"What about emergencies?" C.H. says.

"You've been here for years. I'm sure you can handle any emergencies that come your way."

They seem happy and sad. Happy I don't want to impose, but sad that I don't want to have access, like Lou did. So I add, "As we become closer, over time, I would love to have access to your area. But even so, I won't go beyond the lobby without your permission."

That brings big smiles to their little mouths.

"Want to take a tour?" Curly says.

"Would you like me to?"

"Absolutely!"

"How about you cancel the kill code first?"

Chapter 15

GEEK CITY TURNS out to be six bedrooms, seven bathrooms, a conference room, kitchen, workshop, laundry room, and a computer room that defies explanation. They're music nerds, each possessing a private collection of more than ten thousand songs that blare constantly from breakfast to dinner, at the highest possible volume.

"Do you ever play the same song at the same time?" I ask.

They look at each other and smile. C.H. says, "What a perfect question to ask! Every afternoon at precisely two-forty-six, we play *Dream Merchant*, by Gee Gee Shinn."

Not that I give a shit, but because of the way they're looking at me, I ask, "Why that particular song?"

"The four of us programmed our individual music into our peripheral computers," Larry says. "Day after day for years no two computers ever played the same song at the same time."

C.H. says, "Until eighteen months ago. One afternoon, at two-forty-six, two computers played *Dream Merchant* at the same time."

"Do you know what the odds are of that happening?" C.H. says.

"A million to one?" I say.

Curly yells, "Jimmy Charles! Nineteen sixty!"

Larry shouts, "Patterson, New Jersey!"

C.H. says, "That's nothing. *Nothing!* Who sang backup?" While the others struggle to answer, he yells "The Revellettes!"

"Ah, but who were *in* the Revellettes?" I say.

They look at each other and do a double-take. Then grab their cell phones and punch the keys furiously.

Larry gets there first.

"Jackie and Evelyn Kline—"

Curly and C.H. shout in unison, "And Dottie Hailstock!"

They slap each other on the back, do a high-five, and some sort of strange victory dance.

Then C.H. says, "The odds of two of our lists playing a single song at the same time are impossible to calculate because our lists were pre-programmed to constantly shuffle, and each computer has a different random sequence. We've been working on the calculation for years. I can show you the algorithm flow chart if you'd like."

"Another time," I say, which sets them to laughing.

The biggest surprise comes when they show me Moe's room and I happen to open the closet door and see his corpse hanging from a hook, wrapped in plastic.

"This can't stay here," I say.

"Okay," Curly says.

I supervise as they carry the body to the antechamber.

"How long will you need to keep my laptop?" I ask.

"For what?" Larry says.

"To program it the way I outlined."

"We can do it remotely. We'll send you a link when it's ready."

"We should exchange phone numbers," I say.

They laugh.

"Right," I say. "You've got my number."

"And you've got ours," Larry says. "All you have to do is press the star key twice. We'll answer."

"How will you hear my call over the music?"

"All phone calls mute the music."

We say our goodbyes. When they're out of sight I look at Moe's body, at my feet. A man so broken up by Lou's sudden death, he killed himself. A man so alone in the world there was no one to contact about his death.

Unless the others killed him and made up the story.

I shake my head, call Tommy Cooper, and tell him to bring a friend.

Chapter 16

Callie Carpenter.

THE CONTEMPORARY GANGSTER handbook calls for high income-earners to keep a low community profile. Following that advice to a T, Frankie and Angie De Luca maintain an unassuming home in a modest neighborhood.

It's nine-thirty p.m. under a dark sky as Callie approaches the residence. She knows the De Lucas dined across town with Sal, Marie, and several mob lieutenants and wives at Luigi's, a mob-connected family restaurant. Their plans had been to finish dinner around nine, then watch the fireworks from the restaurant's courtyard, which overlooks the Ohio River. Luigi's isn't the best viewing spot, since the fireworks are launched a mile away, but it's safe, private, and the De Lucas will be there at least another forty-five minutes. Which means they'll be gone an hour, if you include driving time.

And why wouldn't you?

She picks the back door lock so quietly the family dog sleeps through the process.

Until Callie opens the door.

When that happens, several things occur. One. The alarm panel beeps, which tells her the De Lucas have an alarm, but failed to set it. Two. The beep is sufficiently loud to wake the bullmastiff, who goes berserk upon finding a strange woman standing in the hallway. Three. Callie leaps atop the washing machine and spends the next twenty minutes hopping back and forth between the washer and dryer as the dog snarls, lunges, jumps, and tries to eat her ankles instead of the biscuits Callie keeps tossing to the floor.

Callie didn't know there'd be a dog, but there often is, so she came prepared. The dog biscuits contain enough synthetic opiate analgesic to render your typical canine adversary unconscious within minutes.

Dosing is simple.

Each biscuit neutralizes twenty pounds of dog. For a ten-pounder, you break the biscuit in half. The dog currently trying to maim Callie is a seven-biscuit beast.

Ten minutes of jumping tires most bullmastiffs. Twenty minutes exhausts them. When the De Luca mastiff finally hits the wall, he eats the biscuits and hits the floor with a heavy thud.

Callie races to the kitchen and searches the drawers and cabinets till she finds the burglar alarm pamphlet where she rightly assumed the De Lucas recorded their alarm code.

She tests it.

It works.

She thumbs through the pamphlet and learns how to bypass the monitoring company.

She goes to the garage, finds Angie's keys right where she expected to: in the console tray of Angie's car. She removes the door key and slips it in the pocket of her jeans. Then searches the house, finds Frankie's guns, removes the bullets.

Under normal circumstances, killing Angie and Frankie would be child's play. But Creed wants her to torture Frankie, hoping to learn something he can use to justify Frankie's death. If, for example, Creed can prove Frankie's been skimming money, Sal would condone the hit.

She walks back to the laundry room, sits on the floor beside the dog, and strokes his head. This is an ugly-ass dog. First time Callie's ever seen one that's uglier asleep than awake. While Callie isn't opposed to killing animals, she needs a better reason than its appearance. And killing this one would take the De Lucas out of their routine. They'll come home, expect the dog to meet them at the door enthusiastically. If it doesn't, they're going to be concerned. Killing and torturing people works best when you catch them by surprise, while they're following their daily routines. The fewer variables, the better.

If killing the dog's a poor option, not killing him is even worse. He could start barking when Callie returns later tonight. If so, Angie might call the cops. Nothing worse than trying to torture a guy while police bang on the victim's door, demanding to enter.

If she further sedates the dog, the De Lucas will come home, find their pet unconscious. They'll panic, and rush him to the vet.

And Callie would break into an empty house.

The dog has turned this simple killing into a complete cluster fuck.

Creed's original idea had been for Callie to oil the doors, test the floors for sound, and sneak back in at two a.m. while the De Lucas were sleeping. She'd creep into their bedroom, kill Angie quickly, before Frankie can react. Then torture Frankie, gain the information she needs, then kill him.

Callie sighs, removes a tiny disk from her back pack, peels off the backing, and attaches it to the inside of the dog's collar. The disk contains a miniature blasting cap and plastic explosive that can be detonated remotely from Callie's cell phone. Press a button and Fido's head comes clean off.

She pats his head again and says, "I hope it doesn't come to this."

Then she goes into the kitchen and makes herself a sandwich.

Chapter 17

THE DE LUCAS' FRIDGE yields thin-sliced smoked turkey fresh enough to pass her smell test. That, plus mayo and oat nut bread makes a meal. She'd prefer some lettuce and tomato, but beggars can't be choosers. She grabs a bottled water, sits on a barstool by the island in the kitchen, and nibbles her sandwich while deciding what to do about the De Lucas and their dog. That done, her mind drifts to the conference call she received last night from Annie Lorber and Emerson Watkins, whose fathers co-founded Sensory Resources.

"Lou Kelly's dead," Annie said.

After expressing shock, Callie asked what happened.

"You know Rachel Case?"

"Creed's former girlfriend."

"*Former?*" Annie said.

"Forget I said that. What about her?"

"You're aware Lou was dating Rachel Case's mother?"

"Sherry, right? What happened?"

"Apparently Lou and Sherry were infected by the same mercury poisoning Miles Gundy created for his terrorist attack in Memphis."

"How's that possible?"

"We believe Gundy combined dimethylmercury poison with a live HSV-1 virus and placed it on the barre of a dance studio. The dancers were infected on contact."

"Lou was locked away at Sensory Resources, in Virginia."

"He and Sherry went to Roanoke, on a date."

"Still. Roanoke's a long way from Memphis."

"The contagion life cycle was four to five hours. A client took the class in Memphis, flew to Roanoke to visit her sister, and wiped out the whole family. Apparently Lou Kelly or Sherry came into contact with her at some point."

"Wrong place, wrong time?"

"Exactly. But the reason we're calling—"

"Lou's job?"

"Exactly."

"Have you spoken to Donovan Creed?"

"Not yet."

"Why are you calling me? To vouch for his character?"

"No," Emerson said. "We're offering you the position."

Callie laughed. "Creed's the one you need."

"He killed our fathers!" Annie said.

"*What?*"

"We don't know that for certain, Annie," Emerson said.

"Yes we do."

"Please dismiss that," Emerson said. "We're offering you complete control, Miss Carpenter. You'll run the agency, Creed will work for you, should you care to keep him."

Callie laughed.

"What's so funny?"

"Why wouldn't I keep Creed?"

"Keep him, kill him, your choice," Annie says. "I hate the bastard."

"Let me put an end to your anger," Callie said. "Creed didn't kill your father, Annie. Nor yours, Emerson."

"You know that for a fact?" Annie said.

"I do."

"Then who killed him?"

Callie paused. "Tara Siegel."

"Who?"

"She used to work for Sensory."

"Where is she now?"

"Dead."

"What happened to her?"

"I killed her."

"That's awfully convenient."

"Tara might disagree with that comment."

"Still, we have only your word on it."

"And I'm the one you asked. Look, do you think I care if you hate Creed? If you're determined to hate him, there are plenty of legitimate reasons. It's just that killing your father's not one of them."

Emerson says, "Will you accept the position? It's yours for the asking."

"I'll think about it."

"We need to know by ten a.m. tomorrow."

"What happens at ten?"

"We call Creed, to offer him the job."

"Does Creed know Lou's dead?"

"No," Emerson said. "So if he tells you, act surprised."

"Okay."

"That's it?" Annie said. "No thank you?"

"For what?"

"For giving you this opportunity."

Callie laughed. "What do you want me to say? It's a shit job."

Chapter 18

IT ISN'T MUCH of a sandwich, but Callie gets it down, tosses the empty bottle of water in the trash, goes back to the laundry room. She removes the explosive disk from the dog's collar, tosses it in her backpack, takes out a prepared syringe and injects the dog to deepen the dosage. Walks to the nightstand in the master bedroom, where she'd seen Angie's sleeping pills on a People magazine earlier. She bites the top off the plastic medicine bottle and tosses it to the floor, scattering the tiny pills across the carpet. Then she tosses the magazine on the floor and rips several pages from it, puts two pills in her pocket, and two more on the hallway floor by the laundry room. She scatters the magazine pages, inspects her work, and decides it's not quite right, so she wets a paper towel and dabs the pages and pills till they're soggy.

The idea being the De Lucas will come home, find the dog passed out, see the sleeping pills on the floor, think the dog got into the pills and fell asleep. Angie will count the pills she can find and determine two are missing. She'll want to take the dog to the vet, but Frankie will say, "Are you kidding me? Who's gonna carry a hundred and thirty pound dog after drinking all day and half the night? Two pills is nothing! Let him sleep it off."

With any luck, that's what will happen. Callie will hide in the hall closet and wait for the De Lucas to come home. When they fall asleep, she'll make her move. If they freak out over the dog, she'll jump out of the closet, kill them, and manufacture the evidence she needs to convince Sal that Frankie was skimming money.

Since either development requires her to wait in the hall closet for what could be many hours, she goes to the powder room and pees, then enters the closet, removes some coats from their hangers, and positions them on the floor for maximum comfort.

She takes her position among the coats, covers herself with two of them, and runs through her mental checklist. *Did I turn on any lights? If so, did I turn them back off? Check. Did I wipe down all the surfaces I touched in the kitchen and elsewhere? Check. What about the toilet seat? Yup, did that. What about the handle when I flushed? Yup, got that.*

She reminds herself to wipe down both sides of the closet door knob after killing Frankie.

It's pitch black in the closet. She closes her eyes. May as well catch a few minutes of sleep till the De Lucas arrive. When they do, they'll certainly make enough noise to wake her up.

Chapter 19

TIME SLOWS TO a crawl when you're lying on the floor of a coat closet in a strange house waiting to torture and kill the residents.

Callie's trying to drift asleep, but something's tugging at the edge of her awareness. Something that won't go away, drowsy as she is. Something about ... Something she's forgotten.

The closet is pitch black, and has a musty odor from winter clothes that haven't been worn for at least five months. She wonders about silverfish. Centipedes. Spiders crawling around her, possibly on her.

She doesn't like spiders.

If she had her way, there wouldn't be any spiders in the world. If she could somehow lock them all in a giant closet, and blow it up before they have a chance to ...

And there it was.

The thing she forgot to do.

The thing Creed taught her all those years ago. The thing he made her always promise to have in place before getting into position.

An escape plan.

A second way out, in case something goes wrong.

She'd made herself a sitting duck.

No problem, she'll just—

Her thoughts are interrupted by the rumble of a garage door opening. The De Lucas' garage door. Which gives her what, thirty seconds? A minute to create an escape plan?

Not a full minute. No way.

The smart thing would be to stay put. In the eight years she's killed people she's needed an alternate escape plan exactly how many times?

None.

She chose the hall closet for two reasons. One, it contains winter clothes. Who comes home from an all-day Fourth of July party, dinner, fireworks, and checks their winter clothes?

No one.

Reason number two, it's centrally located. The garage, laundry room, kitchen, dining room—are on one end of the house, the master bedroom and bath on the other. The foyer, powder room, and den are close by.

It's the best possible location to hear anything happening in the whole house. The perfect place to hide and wait.

It's ten-twenty at night in the middle of the summer. The De Lucas are tired and hot. They won't open the winter clothes closet. And even if they did, she's on the floor, covered up, with a gun in her hand. She could blow them away before the surprise registers on their faces.

She'll be fine.

Unless Frankie invited his crew members over for a drink!

Half his gang was in town for Sal's party. Why *wouldn't* he have them swing by for some late night drinks, maybe run a little strategy session? The wives could chat in the kitchen, the guys could meet in the den or basement.

Callie shakes her head in disbelief. How could this have gotten past her?

She's holding a single gun, seven rounds. Has a vial of lens spray in the back pocket of her jeans. If things go south she'll have to move quickly, rush her shots. Four guys caught unaware?

She's Callie Carpenter. Likes her chances.

Five guys? Too close to call.

Seven? Out of the question.

There are worse places to die than Frankie's house, worse ways to die than a mob shootout. What sucks is how easily she could have avoided this predicament.

She tells herself not to worry. It's late. The De Lucas have partied all day. They'll be alone.

But what if they're not?

If the entire crew's here, she'll die tonight.

If Frankie's crew shows up.

If they find her.

It all comes down to the dog. If he wakes up, he'll sniff her out.

She hears the garage door closing again, hears car doors slam. How many?

Two doors. One car.

So far so good.

And where do mobsters meet, anyway? In the boss's home?

No.

They meet in clubs, offices, strip joints.

Except when their wives are in town.

In which case this is exactly where they'd come.

Shit!

Is it likely Frankie's crew is coming?

No.

But what if they do?

Callie always provides for every possibility.

Always.

But not this time. True, she didn't come to Sal's party expecting to kill a mobster and his wife tonight.

But still. How basic is this?

A fucking escape plan in case things go wrong.

She's made mistakes before, obviously, but none like this. She's clearly off her game.

Which reminds her of something else that happened today. Something monumental. Something she thought couldn't happen in a million years.

She found a weakness in Donovan Creed!

A weakness that could be exploited.

Angie's in the garage now, making loud baby talk. Like she's teasing the dog, expecting him to squeal with delight that she's home. It's the sort of baby talk women do when they have an audience.

Callie's mind goes to warp speed. If she *had* created an alternate escape plan, what would it be?

She wills herself to focus ...

And gets it.

If she had a mere minute to prepare, she could do it.

But she doesn't.

She'd place explosive disks at strategic places in the house, waist-high, and program her cell phone to blow them simultaneously. The disks have a sticky backing that adheres to walls, and offers a kill zone of six feet. Using the hall closet door as the center point, she would set two disks in the hallway, twelve feet apart. They'd blow outward and sideways, and wipe out everyone within twenty-four feet. The closet door and interior walls would provide enough protection to keep her unscathed.

Four other disks could have been set along her escape route. The sudden carnage would kill anyone in the hallway, and injure or stun anyone between her and the back door.

That's what she *could* have done, but didn't.

She hears the garage door open. Angie cooing, "Are you hungry, honey bear? Is mama's little baby hungry?"

Frankie, still in the garage saying, "What, you expect him to answer? *Yeah, mama, I'm hungry! I'm so fuckin' hungry, mama!*"

Is he showing off for his crew members? Callie strains to hear outside laughter, but only hears Angie say, "Oh, shut up, asshole!"

Which allows her to relax. Angie would never speak to him like that if others were present.

Making a mental note to be more careful next time, she puts her head back down, covers it with a coat, and eases into her deep relaxation zone, which she'll maintain till the De Lucas are sleeping soundly.

Everything seems great. Until Angie screams.

"What the *fuck?*" Frankie yells.

"*Call the cops!*"

"What?"

"Call the cops!"

"Why?"

"Someone's in the house!"

Chapter 20

AS THE ADRENALIN surges through her veins, Callie wonders what tipped Angie off. The unconscious dog? The fact the alarm didn't beep when they opened the door? She grabs her gun and jumps to her feet as Angie yells, "Look!"

Callie quietly opens the closet door, hears Frankie shout, "What the fuck happened?"

By the time Angie yells "They've killed Digby!" Callie's made her way down the hall. She comes up behind the De Lucas as Angie's kneeling over the dog, and Frankie's opened his cell phone, ready to dial 911.

"Digby's okay," Callie says.

"Jesus *Christ*!" Frankie yells, startled.

Angie screams and tries to lunge at Callie. But Callie's got a gun in one hand and a tiny vial of lens cleaner in the other. She sprays the lens cleaner into Angie's face. Of course, it's not lens cleaner at all. It's just packaged that way. To the world, it's a small metal cylinder, silver, with the words

"Lens Cleaner" printed in black. But this particular cylinder contains a mixture of cyanide and dimethyl sulfoxide.

Angie screams and tries to get to her feet, but falls face-first to the floor. Meanwhile, Frankie's in mid-air, diving toward Callie's knees. Unable to get off a shot, she clubs him over the head with the butt of the gun as he tackles her. She lands hard on her back, with him on top. She feels the wind go out of her as his head crashes into her stomach. Frankie's hurt, but he's tough, and has Callie pinned beneath him. She's still holding the gun, but with the silencer attached, it's too long to wedge between them for a shot. Frankie gets to his knees and cocks his fist. Is he planning to shatter her perfect nose?

Yes.

Does he?

No.

She drops the gun, and Frankie lunges for it.

Just as she hoped he would.

When he makes his move, she twists her body enough to slide out from under him. He stretches out to grab the gun, but Callie gets her elbow above the back of his head and smashes his face to the floor. Then scrambles to her feet and kicks his ribs.

Frankie's tough. He never loses his grip on the gun, and turns it on her. Callie kicks his hand, sends the gun flying. As he watches it sail through the air, she lands a front kick to his temple. Frankie goes dizzy. His head goes upward, exposing his jaw. When she connects with a roundhouse kick, it's lights out Frankie.

Chapter 21

"WHAT TIPPED HER off?" Creed says, hours later, when Callie gets to that part of the story.

Callie laughs. "You're going to think I'm an idiot."

"Tell me."

"The washer and dryer."

"What about them?"

"They were covered with scratch marks!"

Creed laughs. "Of course. Twenty minutes of hopping from one appliance to the other, with the dog trying to get you!"

"And I never even noticed," Callie says, "or thought about it. But to Angie, it must've looked like a war zone!"

"Especially with her dog lying unconscious on the floor."

"Digby."

"Right," Creed says. "So ..."

"So what?"

"Tell me what happened with Frankie."

Chapter 22

Two Hours Earlier ...

FRANKIE REGAINS CONSCIOUSNESS in gradual stages of ascending violence. When he's lucid enough to realize he's on his back with his wrists and ankles securely tied, he screams bloody murder. Callie turns the lights on so he can see what he's up against.

Cheesecloth.

She's holding a small wad of cheesecloth in one hand and a kitchen knife in the other. Puts the knife blade against his lips.

"Open up," Callie says, cheerfully.

"Fuck you!"

She moves the knife tip a few centimeters to the right and jabs it into his cheek. When he yells to protest, she pushes the center part of the cheese cloth into his mouth. When he gags, she forces the knife in his mouth and presses the blade against his tongue to keep him from spitting out the cheesecloth.

He yells and bucks his body, but wisely keeps his head still.

"Hot?" she says.

Frankie makes a pain sound. His eyes bug out. Tears collect in the corners of his eyes and drip down his cheeks.

"You're tasting distilled habanero," Callie says, "from the Chili pepper. In its purest form, the habanero tops three hundred and fifty thousand Scoville heat units. Very few people can handle this type of heat on their tongues, and it's clear you're not one of them."

"*Uhhhnnn! UHHHNNN!*" He cries out. It's the only pain sound he can make without hurting himself worse.

She sighs. "I won't lie to you, Frankie, you're in for a bad time. Because while this seems blisteringly hot to you, it's the weakest extract I brought. And I brought many."

She lets the heat intensify another thirty seconds, then says, "Okay. Unclench your jaw and I'll remove it."

"W-water!" he gasps.

Callie says, "You're eyes are tearing up. Here, let me help you."

He closes his eyes so she can wipe them. She does, but when he opens them again, he sees her holding a medicine dropper above his left eye. Before he can blink, she squirts something in his eye that makes him shriek in pain.

"That's what it feels like in your eyes," she says. "In liquid form."

He blinks his eyes and shakes his head from side to side in super speed, like an old cartoon character in distress.

"AHH! AHH! AHH!" he yells, reminding her of a guy she interrogated years ago, before she began packing torture kits in her backpack. That day she boiled a pot of water and poured it on his bare skin a cup at a time. He made this same sound, Ahh! Ahh! Ahh!

When Frankie stops shaking his head he focuses his good eye on the medicine dropper, unaware of what's in Callie's left hand.

A second swab of cheesecloth.

The center of which she stuffs in his mouth.

She holds her left hand over his lips to keep it in place.

Frankie makes a moaning sound.

Callie says, "You're bluffing. You can't feel the heat this time. Not yet, anyway. But give it another fifteen seconds and see how you feel. While we wait, I'll tell you that what's in your mouth is a Bhut Jolokia pepper, which, only a few years ago, was considered the hottest pepper in the world. DNA tests confirmed it's an interspecies hybrid of Capsicum chinense and frutescens genes."

The involuntary spasms contorting Frankie's body tell her he's begun to feel the heat.

She squirts some in his right eye, saying, "This little baby packs one million Scoville heat units. Can you believe it?"

He can.

Frankie shrieks like a wounded wolverine. His body feels like it's shutting down.

Callie removes the cheesecloth from his mouth.

After a full minute of blubbering, he forms the words, "Wh-what do you *w-want?*""You know what really pisses me off?" she says. "You haven't even bothered to ask about your wife."

"Wh-what have y-you ... wh-what's h-happened to An-An-Angie?" he sputters.

"She's resting quietly," Callie says. "Thanks for asking."

"P-please," he says. "S-Stop!"

"Frankie, listen to me. In a few minutes I'm going to ask you some questions. You'll want to answer them because I've got lots of these vials, and trust me, some are particularly nasty."

A few feet away, on the laundry room floor, Digby starts twitching. Callie shakes her head and says, "Your dog is getting on my nerves."

She removes the syringe from her backpack and gives Digby another dose. Then puts it up and gets another length of cheesecloth and says, "Open your mouth, Frankie."

"N-no! Ask y-your qu-questions. I'll tell you wh-whatever you w-want to know."

"Not yet. You need to know how bad this can get. Will you open your mouth for me? Or no?"

He shakes his head.

"I figured you'd say that."

She removes a can of lighter fluid from her backpack and a long-stemmed lighter. Squirts the fluid on his crotch and sets his pants on fire.

When he opens his mouth to scream she stuffs another swatch of cheesecloth in it. He bucks his body up and down and twists from side to side. Tries to spit the cloth out, but his lips, mouth, and tongue won't cooperate. They're blistered and raw.

"I'm going to let your pants burn for a minute, Frankie, while I tell you about the Naga Viper. This is an unstable hybrid of three peppers. A devil's trifecta, if you will."

She squirts some in his left eye and he begins speaking in tongues.

"This one registers one-point-four million heat units."

She notices he's wet his pants.

"You put the fire out all by yourself!" she says. "That was really clever."

Callie feels her cell phone vibrating softly in her pants pocket. She opens it, reads the text message. *Call me. Midnight?*

She smiles, texts "Yes," closes the phone, puts it back in her pocket. Then she unbuckles Frankie's belt, pulls his smoldering pants and boxers down to his knees.

She says, "I'd hold still if I were you."

She uses the knife's sharp edge to scrape a layer of skin off his nuts. Then she opens the vial of Naga Viper extract and pours it on his nuts, and Frankie goes unconscious.

When he comes to she says, "Now that I've got your attention, I hope you'll believe me when I tell you I've got two more vials. One is the Trinidad Moruga Scorpion, the current world's hottest pepper. It weighs in at over two million heat units. The other is pure capsaicin, a hydrophobic compound that registers a whopping sixteen million Scoville. If that doesn't get you talking, I'll dump a jar of acid on your penis. It's really up to you."

"Please," he begs. "Put the fire out."

"The fire's out."

"No. It's burning the skin off my nuts. You're killing me! I'm gonna die!"

"You're just feeling the after-effects of the liquid pepper extract. This is why you don't want me to open the bad vials."

"P-please. Check for f-flames. M-My skin's on fire!"

"I'm looking, Frankie. I know it hurts. That's why they call it torture. But your balls are blistered, that's all. So, will you talk to me?"

He nods.

"Good boy. You know Donovan Creed?"

Frankie nods.

"He was hoping to be here. And no better than you've handled this? You're getting off light. But while I'm more civilized than Creed, I'm just as determined to make you talk. Do you understand?"

"I'll talk."

"Good, 'cause you're one squirt away from losing your eyesight."

"P-please!"

"Creed says you're skimming money."

"No. I would never—what are you doing?"

She opens the vial of Trinidad Moruga Scorpion ...

"*No!*"

... And pours it up and down the length of his penis.

And Frankie cries. Sobs like a child.

When at last he settles down, Callie says, "You're not going to make me use the pure cap, are you?"

"Drugs," he says.

"What about them?"

"I'm selling drugs on the side."

"What type of drugs?"

"Heroin."

"Who's your contact?"

He shakes his head.

Callie reaches for the vial of pure capsaicin and says, "I'll remind you. This is eight times worse than the last one. And I've got to say, your penis isn't looking very happy."

She starts to open the vial.

"Wait!" he says.

She pauses.

"Are you going to kill me anyway?"

"That depends."

"On what?"

"On you giving me the right answers. I know you don't trust me, so I'm going to tell you a little secret. Sal hired Creed to kill Angie, not you. Sal doesn't know you've been skimming. Creed planned to kill Angie, then torture you until he got a reason to justify your death to Sal. If Creed hadn't been called away on business, you'd both be dead by now."

"But you work for Creed."

"Well, here's the thing. Creed and I work for the government. They've offered me the top job. I said no, so they're giving it to Creed. So I'm thinking, maybe I tell Creed I tortured you and couldn't get anything because you're clean. So I spare your life. Meanwhile, you cut me in on your drug deal."

"What about Angie?"

"She's resting quietly."

"But what about her? Are you going to kill her?"

Callie sighs. "I can't protect her. She's been saying things that could bring down the whole organization."

"I know. Shit. I told her to stop, but she can't keep her fuckin' mouth shut. She hears shit, she tells it. But still. She's my wife. Maybe I can talk to Sal, get him to give her another chance."

"Sorry. That's not part of the deal."

"But I love her, you know? I can't bear to watch her suffer."

"I understand. Look, if it makes you feel any better, she's been dead for the past twenty minutes."

Chapter 23

Donovan Creed.
Sensory Resources, Virginia.

"SO AFTER YOU told him Angie was dead, what did he do?" I ask.

Callie says, "He gave me the name of his drug contact."

"Is it someone we know?"

"Oh, yes indeed."

"Were you surprised?"

"Stunned," she says.

"Am I going to be stunned?"

"You, sir, are going to shit."

"Tell me."

Chapter 24

"BRACE YOURSELF," CALLIE says.

"Enough buildup," I say. "Who's Frankie's drug contact?"

"Sophie Alexander."

"*What?* No shit?"

"That's what I said to Frankie!"

"Sal's niece?" I say.

"The same."

"Wow!"

"I said that too!" Callie says.

I visited Sophie's home in Nashville last month while posing as an FBI agent. I was there to observe the agency's interrogation of Dani for the murder of her husband. At the time, Dani didn't know me, but Sophie and I spoke in private, which gave me the opportunity to walk through her home. It was modest on the outside, but the furniture and wall hangings suggested an income beyond what she earned from writing songs. At the time I thought she might be hooking, or selling some weed on the side. But the idea Sophie might be higher up the drug ladder than Frankie De Luca?

Astonishing.

"Hello? Did you fall asleep?" Callie asks.

"Why, you got a flight to catch?"

"I try to stay busy."

"It's after midnight."

"We're not all a hundred years old."

"Sad, but true. Did Frankie give you details?"

"Sophie's a mule. She meets a guy in a different hotel in a different city each month. Depends on where she's performing. The guy brings her a suitcase full of H. At some point over the next few days she meets Frankie at a pre-determined spot. They exchange suitcases."

"So Frankie gets next month's heroin, Sophie gets last month's cash."

"That's right."

"I've never heard of anyone in the drug trade waiting a whole month for payment."

"She must be dealing with someone at the very top."

"I don't suppose Frankie gave you a name?"

"He didn't know any names."

"You're certain?"

"Quite."

"You asked with extreme prejudice?"

"You know I did. So, are you going to tell Sal about his precious niece?"

"That depends."

"On what?"

"Did you kill Frankie?"

"Did you tell me to?"

"Yes." He pauses. Then says, "And you did?"

Callie chuckles. "Yes, Donovan. I killed Frankie. He was in a lot of pain. It was a mercy killing."

"Then yes, we need to tell Sal. Sooner, not later."

"*We?*"

"What happened to the dog?"

"Digby's alive and well. I set out some food and water, and moved the bodies so he won't be too upset when he comes to. If he's not found by ten tomorrow, I'll place an anonymous call to the police."

"That's a lot of trouble to go to. Are you going soft on me?"

"I couldn't bear to kill such an ugly dog."

"No cameras? No surveillance equipment?"

"None."

"You find that odd?"

"Not really. Sal's pretty adamant that his lieutenants keep a low profile."

"I agree. But speaking of Sal, we need to tell him."

"That's the second time you said 'we.' What am I missing?"

"Now that I've got this new job, I'm hoping you'll decide to work with me."

"I already work with you."

"I mean together. You and me."

"Sorry, I'm not sure I understand."

"I want you to help me run Sensory. We'll work out of the office together."

"It's a shit job."

"Currently, yes. But it doesn't have to be."

"You've got plans?"

"Lots."

"Does the committee know about your plans?"

I laugh out loud. "What do you think?"

"I think it's hilarious. You've been on the job a few hours and you're already fucking the system. I'm all for it. But you're forgetting something."

"What's that?"

"My penthouse in Vegas."

"So? I'm opening a spa and surgery center in Vegas."

"What I'm saying, I'm not moving to Virginia."

"Me either. I'm moving Sensory to Vegas."

"You can do that?"

"We'll have two locations. One for geeks, one for freaks."

"Freaks?"

"I was channeling my inner rap star."

"What does that mean?"

"Geeks? Freaks? It's a rhyme. See, what I was going for is—"

"Donovan?"

"Yeah?"

"Keep your day job."

"Okay."

Chapter 25

Las Vegas.
Gwen Peters.

"LET'S SEE IF I've got this straight," Gwen Peters says. "You're offering me five hundred dollars to meet you for a cup of coffee?"

"That's right."

"And Carmine Porello gave you my cell phone number?"

"That's correct."

"Tell him I'm not interested."

"Five hundred dollars for ten minutes of your time," the young lady says.

"If Carmine's paying, make it a grand. But the answer's still going to be no."

"I'll agree to the thousand," she says. "When can we meet?"

Gwen pauses. "What did you say your name was?"

"Willow Breeland. And it's not Carmine's money, it's mine."

"What's going on here, Ms. Breeland? Are you trying to set me up?"

"No. And you can call me Willow. I'm only eighteen."

"It has to be a public place."

"No problem."

"What is it you want?"

"I'm the new girl."

"At Club Six?"

"The same. Carmine talks about you all the time. I want to meet you and find out why."

Gwen laughs. "You're ambitious."

"You have no idea."

"I'll make this easy. You know the Starbucks on Emerson and Valley View?"

"No, but I'll find it."

"Find it quick. I'll be there in twenty minutes."

"How will I know you?"

Gwen laughs. "You'll know me!" She pauses, then says. "And I'll know you, too."

Gwen was right. When she enters the coffee shop twenty minutes later, a pretty young woman stands.

Gwen walks to her table and says, "Willow?"

"Hi, Gwen."

She sits down, motions Gwen to do the same.

"You have something for me?" Gwen says.

Willow removes an envelope from her handbag, pushes it across the table.

"Please," she says. "Have a seat."

Gwen sits, picks up the envelope, lifts the flap, smiles.

"You're certainly one of a kind!" she says.

"Thank you."

Gwen looks at her watch. "Your ten minutes starts ... right now. What do you want to know?"

"Let's start with Roy."

"What about him?"

"Is he capable of bringing down Carmine?"

"With the right backing."

"Then why hasn't he?"

Gwen starts to answer, then pauses. She looks around the room, carefully studying the customers. Finally she says, "Are you wearing a wire?"

"No, of course not!"

Gwen studies her a minute, then says, "Let's go."

"Where?"

"Rest room."

"Why?"

"If you're planning to ask me mob shit, you'll have to prove you're not wearing a wire."

"Wait. You don't mean—"

Gwen laughs. "That's *exactly* what I mean!"

Chapter 26

"WELL, THIS IS embarrassing," Willow says, as she lowers her panties to mid-thigh and turns in a circle.

"Oh please," Gwen says. "You're a stripper. Now bend over and spread your cheeks."

"Really, Gwen? Because I think not."

Gwen laughs. "I just wanted to see how far you'd go."

They're standing in the middle of the restroom at Starbucks. Willow, buck naked, save for the panties at her thighs.

"Can I get dressed now? Because I won't know what to say if some random customer walks in here with a little girl."

"Relax. It's nine-thirty at night." Gwen turns on both faucets and lets them run. She motions Willow to come closer. Then whispers, "If you want to ask me about the mob, do it now."

"Why hasn't Roy tried to take over the business from Carmine?"

"Have you ever heard of a guy named Donovan Creed?"

"No."

"He's a hit man for the mob. From what I hear, Roy was about to make a move on Carmine. The night before, Creed showed up in the club and saw Roy disrespecting Carmine. He gave him a lecture about it, and crushed Roy's hand to show he's serious. That one action saved Carmine's life."

"Who was helping Roy take Carmine's down?"

"I don't know. Why do you care?"

"I want to bet on the right horse."

"And here I thought you wanted to talk me into coming back to the Top Six!"

"I do. But not as a stripper."

"I don't understand."

"I want you to take over Roy's job."

"*Excuse me?*"

"You're a legend in the business, and Carmine loves you. I think he'd pay you a hundred grand to run the girls. Who could possibly handle the girls better than a former stripper?"

"True. But Carmine doesn't have the guts, or the power to fire Roy."

"I'll take care of Roy."

"How?"

"Can you keep a secret?"

"Of course."

"I'm going to kill him."

"You?"

"Uh huh."

"Personally?"

"I'd prefer to pay someone else to do it, but I'll do it if I have to."

"How?"

"I'm not sure yet. But I'll find a way to make it happen."

Gwen shakes her head in disbelief. Willow's obviously crazy. But there's something about her that fosters confidence.

After a moment of silence, Gwen says "I might know someone."

"Your girlfriend?"

Gwen says, "Carmine told you about Callie?"

"You'd be amazed how much information I can extract from a single blow job."

"Eew! Sorry, but ... *Carmine?*"

Willow laughs. "I know, I know."

"Jesus, Willow. He's what, seventy-five?"

"Try seventy-eight."

"Eew."

"It's not that bad. You've just got to get your head in the game. No pun intended."

"I couldn't make myself do it. I'd gag and retch. You know those disgusting things they make you eat on Survivor?"

"Yeah?"

"It would be like that."

Willow laughs. "Well, I'm certainly no expert on dicks. But in my limited experience they all taste pretty much the same. Blindfolded, I wouldn't be able to distinguish between Brad Pitt and the Three Stooges."

"No offense, but you sound pretty experienced to me."

"I've blown a total of four guys if you include Carmine and my step-father."

"Omigod! Your step-father?"

"Not all blow jobs are by design."

"Wow. I'm sorry."

Willow shrugs. "Water under the bridge."

"You're pretty stoic about it."

"They call it a blow job for a reason. It's a job. A chore. Something no one wants to do on a regular basis. But if you're selective, it can be one of the highest-paying jobs around. If I'm a painter, welder, school teacher, or waitress, I'm working eight hours a day, on my feet, eyes open. And what's the reward? A meager salary from which the government takes thirty-five percent. Or I can blow Carmine for ten minutes a day with my eyes closed. In return, he gives me a twelve hundred dollar-a-month apartment, a car, and two hundred fifty bucks a week for living expenses. He's with his family on Sundays, so I'm on call six days a week. That's the equivalent of getting a thousand bucks a week for an hour of actual work. Of course, I choose to spend a couple hours a day talking to him, but that's a separate investment."

"I never thought of it like that," Gwen says. "Where do I sign up?"

"Gwen, seriously. If you and I team up there's no limit to what we can accomplish."

"I admire your ability to dream big."

"It all starts with the first step. I'm in with Carmine. Second step, Roy. You think Callie will kill Roy for us?"

"Not even."

"Why not? It's how she makes her living."

"She wouldn't want me working there. But can I tell you something?"

"Sure."

"I'm not gay. And although it's a great lifestyle, the handwriting's on the wall."

"What do you mean?"

"I'm a kept woman, we're drifting apart. I can tell she's going to dump me soon."

"Why?"

"I begged her to take me with her this weekend to a big party in Cincinnati. She refused."

"Bad sign."

"I know, right?" Gwen says.

"A hundred grand would make you an independent woman of means."

Gwen laughs. "'Woman of means?' Who talks like that?"

She laughs again. Then says, "Anyway, I'd need more than a hundred grand to leave Callie."

"What if I gave you a piece of the club?"

"*Excuse* me? No offense, Willow, but you're still at square one. You may have big plans, but at the moment, if we're keeping it real, you're a cocksucker. You might be blowing the boss, but *he* owns the club, not you."

For a split second Willow's jaw clenches in anger. But she works through the insult and says, "A year from now you won't remember how I started."

"Meaning?"

"I'm going to leverage my sexual skills into an ownership position."

"You're crazy. He'd never give you his club."

Willow waves her hand dismissively. "No. But under the right circumstances he'll sell me forty-five percent."

"Math was never my best subject," Gwen says, "but I'm pretty sure it takes fifty-one percent ownership to have control."

"In the real world it only takes fifty and the hyphen to control a fifty-fifty deal. I'll own forty-five percent, you'll own five, which gives us fifty."

"And the hyphen?"

"You and the girls."

"Tell me why."

"Working together, you and I will double the value of his business. We'll be running all the day-to-day leaving him to wonder when to take his next dump. If he doesn't like something I've planned, you'll stick up for me. And I'll do the same for you. I'll work the books, you'll work the girls, and Carmine will get fatter, older, and richer. At some point I give him papers to sign, allowing me to legally make all the business decisions. At that point he can either sign the papers, or watch us go down the road and start our own club."

"Wow."

"Trust me, Gwen. For all intents and purposes we'll control that piss ant club in the space of six months. But that's just the first step."

"What do you mean?"

"I want it all."

"There's only one club, Willow."

"Carmine's ripe for the plucking. I want to take over his other businesses."

"Excuse me?"

"I want to run the entire west coast."

Gwen laughs. "You're not even Italian!"

"It's a different era, Gwen. It's all about making money, moving product. Mob guys are like all other guys, meaning they want two things. Money and power. Those who want money will get more. Those who want power will get killed. Are you with me or not?"

"You're eighteen fucking years old! They'll squash you like a bug!"

"When the transition's complete, I'll give you fifty percent of the club. And five percent of everything else."

"You're truly insane."

"Pretend I can do it. Would you run the girls?"

"For five percent ownership?"

"And a hundred grand off the top."

"I don't believe for a minute you can pull this off."

"But if I can?"

"If you can somehow manage to get legal control of the club, yes, I'll run the girls."

Willow smiles. "If you agree to run the girls, I'll get control of the club."

"What do you mean?"

"It's a process. I've known Carmine a few hours and already got his name on an apartment lease. But I have to show him I can deliver. Killing Roy and bringing you back to the club is a hell of a coup."

"Okay, I get that. But I don't understand how you plan to take control."

"Baby steps. First? Lover. Second? Confidante. Third? Business advisor. Fourth? Accountant. Fifth? Well, that depends on what I discover along the way. I'll help you get your hundred grand immediately. And later on, you'll help me gain control. But of course, none of this can happen until—"

"Roy's out of the picture."

"Exactly. So I need to take him out, or find someone who does this sort of thing for a living. It would be nice to have a hit man in my pocket. You think this Donovan Creed guy would do it?"

"No. But I know someone who will."

"Who?"

"Donovan Creed's daughter."

"Seriously?"

Gwen laughs. "You'll have to be careful. She's not playing with a full deck."

"She sounds perfect."

Gwen laughs. "You're a piece of work."

"Can you set up a meeting? First thing tomorrow morning?"

"I'll do my best."

"Great."

"Anything else?"

"Yes."

"What?"

"Can I get dressed now?"

Chapter 27

Callie Carpenter.
Cincinnati.

THE PHONE RINGS five times before Dani answers.

"Hello?"

"Sorry I'm late calling you back," Callie says.

Dani yawns. "That's okay. Can we talk a minute?"

"Yes."

"Um ... where are you?"

"Down the hall."

Callie hears her take a deep breath.

Then Dani says, "You want me to come to your room?"

"No. I'll come to you."

Chapter 28

Callie and Dani.

"I ALMOST GAVE up on you," Dani says.

"I was tied up."

"Not literally, I hope!"

As she enters Dani's room, Callie picks up the scent of perfume. She notices a capless tube of toothpaste on the sink, a wet toothbrush, and a makeup case whose contents are scattered across the counter as if a bomb exploded nearby. Her room has a king bed, a utility desk, and a table with two chairs.

Dani sits at the foot of the bed. Her lips are glossed, her hair freshly-brushed. She's wearing a man's white dress shirt and, from the glimpse Callie got when Dani plopped onto the bed—white cotton panties. Callie slides one of the chairs directly in front of her, and sits in it. From the way the bed's been hastily made, Callie concludes Dani had been sound asleep when she answered the phone. The call ended a minute ago, which means in that small space of time Dani managed to throw the bed together, brush her teeth and hair, and apply perfume and lip gloss, though she had to dump all the makeup out to find the lip gloss.

Callie's in jeans and a scoop-neck tank top, no bra. Their knees are two feet apart.

"How did you know which hotel?" Dani says.

"I started with the closest ones to Sal's house and called till I found you."

"How many did you call?"

"Four."

"I'm impressed."

"What happened tonight?" Callie says.

"We had a fight."

Callie nods. "You want to talk about it?"

Dani smiles. "You'd do that?"

"What?"

"Listen to me rattle on and on about some meaningless fight?"

"If it would make you feel better, yes."

"I wouldn't put you through that."

"Thanks."

Dani laughs.

They're both quiet a minute, Dani staring at her hands in her lap, Callie, staring at Dani. Callie, reading all the signals, knows a slam dunk when she sees one. This incredible creature, Dani Ripper, is primed and ready. All Callie has to do is...

Dani suddenly blurts, "I'm not quite sure how this sort of thing works."

The smile in Callie's heart spreads to her face as she thinks, *how adorable is that!*

Callie silently studies the flawless, insanely desirable woman sitting on the bed a few feet away, who represents everything Callie has ever wanted in a woman, or hoped for. This is Callie's wildest fantasy coming true.

Only Dani's not just ready, she's ready to explode! Her face and neck have bloomed to a crimson flush of passion, even as she struggles to overcome her natural shyness. She wants it, Callie knows, and wants it bad. And what makes the situation even more thrilling and intoxicating is they both know Dani wants Callie to ravage her, and take her to places she's never been. She's not looking for goose bumps. She's looking for a multi-orgasmic crescendo.

Callie can tell Dani's ready to surrender her body to pure passion and desire, that she fully expects to be rendered physically and emotionally spent, like a wet wash cloth that's served its purpose and been wrung so thoroughly there's not a drop of moisture left in it. A wash cloth that, moments after being hung up to dry, drops to the shower floor and stays there, content to steep in the remnant puddles.

Callie understands. She's spent her whole life searching for someone she can touch and be touched by who makes her feel warm and safe inside. Someone who's been through the same hell she's endured. Someone who's experienced the brutality of a man first hand. Someone who, like Callie, had her childhood ripped from her at a tender age.

Dani raises her head and looks at her, and Callie wonders how it's possible for a woman to have such enormous eyes, and why they look beautiful instead of freakish.

Dani places her hands a foot behind her on the bed, for support, and leans back. The sudden movement shows Callie that Dani's braless.

She scoots her chair back a foot to give her something to do besides jumping Dani's bones. But Dani's legs are slightly apart, and from this vantage point a wet spot on her panties comes into view.

Chapter 29

CALLI'ES PULSE QUICKENS. Her breathing gets heavy. She notes every movement Dani makes is more seductive than the previous one, leaving her to conclude Dani isn't half as innocent as she presumed.

Under normal circumstances, Callie would be on this woman like smoke on an oil fire. But the circumstances aren't normal, and Callie feels inexplicably conflicted.

Because of two words Creed uttered.

Not yet.

And because she slapped him.

This morning Callie told Creed she knew what she wanted for her birthday, meaning sex with Dani. Now it's hers for the taking. But she also asked Creed if he'd ever been with a woman as gorgeous as Dani, and Creed looked at her with a twinkle in his eyes and said, "Not yet."

His expression. His words. His tone of voice made it clear he was talking about Callie, not Dani. Yes, he was flirting, as he always does, but this time it was different. It was just two words, but they stuck with her.

And it's these two words that are holding her back even as her body screams at her to get up close and personal with Dani Ripper.

Callie's confused by how suddenly her feelings for Creed have taken over her emotions. On the one hand, there's Creed, and he's not here. On the other, Dani, and she's not only here, she's wet with desire. This is a once-in-a-lifetime opportunity with a one-in-a-million woman. Dani's the kind of woman kings would wage wars over. A keeper. The kind of woman you settle down with. The kind you never want to leave.

"Creed's not gay," Callie says.

"Excuse me?"

"Donovan Creed. He's not gay."

Dani sits up and frowns. "I don't understand."

"I was cock-blocking him."

"I don't know what that means."

"It means you're magnificent. I thought you might be interested in him, so I said he was gay. I wanted to keep you away from him."

Dani allows the comment to hang heavy in the air as she studies its implication.

"You're in love with him."

"Yes."

Dani's voice turns angry. "When did you come to this conclusion, Callie? Before or after you told me you wanted me more than you've ever wanted another woman?"

"Both. But I didn't realize he felt the same way till after."

"You're saying he very recently proclaimed his love for you?"

"He didn't tell me. He *showed* me."

"I don't understand."

"Tonight, before calling you, I found myself in a very dangerous situation, one I could have easily avoided."

"How?"

"That's not important. What's important is I royally fucked up and it could have cost me my life. Which means my head wasn't in the game. And I think it's because I slapped Creed."

"You slapped him."

"Yes."

"When?"

"At the party this morning."

"Why?"

"I don't know. I just did. I told him to be careful, then I slapped him. But that part's not important, either. What's important is I caught him completely unaware."

"You slapped him for no reason?"

"Yup. Slapped the shit out of him."

"I guess in your world that's something to be proud of? Slapping a man's face for no reason?"

"You don't understand."

"You're right."

"I've got incredibly fast hands," Callie says. "I can catch a fly in mid-flight by its feet."

"Its feet?"

"Or its wings, if you prefer."

"I'm not sure I'd have a preference either way."

"The point is, no one's faster than Creed. He's got the reflexes of a mongoose. If I would've tried to slap him a month ago, he would've blocked my hand, or moved his face out of the way."

"But not today."

"No."

"And that tells you something."

"It tells me he loves me."

Dani shakes her head. "I can't believe I hesitated to tell you about my argument with Sophie. At least our fight makes sense."

Callie says, "I think Creed was off his game today because of me."

"Because he loves you?"

"Yes."

"And the reason he loves you is because if he didn't, he would have blocked your hand when you tried to strike him?"

"Exactly."

"But you also said his best friend died, and he was being offered a huge job."

"So?"

"Maybe that's what threw him off his game."

Callie frowns.

Dani says, "You say you're off your game because of your feelings for Creed."

"Yes."

"But you loved him long before today."

Callie nods.

"And yet tonight is the very first time you've ever been off your game."

"So?"

"How do you know you weren't off your game because of us?"

"Us?"

"You and me. You were hoping I'd call you tonight. At least, that's what you said."

Callie frowns again. "You must be one hell of a great detective."

Dani unbuttons her shirt.

Callie says, "What are you doing?"

"Why do you care? You love Creed, he loves you."

"Well, I certainly love him."

"But he might not love you."

"He might not."

"Sophie and I might love each other too, but you thought lustful sex would be good for me. At least, that's what you said."

"I did say that."

"I notice you're staring at my boobs," Dani says. "And your face is flushed. You know what I think?"

"What?"

"I think we should make love tonight, and let tomorrow take care of itself."

"What do you mean?"

"Tomorrow Sophie and I will make up, break up, or stay the same. And your relationship with Donovan will likewise get stronger, weaker, or stay the same."

"What if tomorrow we decide to be together for the rest of our lives?" Callie says.

"Is there much hope of that happening tomorrow?"

"No. But what if it does?"

"In the unlikely event he suddenly proclaims his undying love for you tomorrow, you'll have a happy memory of tonight being your last fling as a single woman."

As she says that, she removes her shirt, scoots onto the center of the bed, lies down, spreads her legs.

She's still wearing panties, but they're sopping wet.

As are Callie's. She grabs her cell phone and presses a button.

Creed answers, "What's wrong?"

"Plenty," Callie says. "You and I are going to settle this once and for all."

"Settle what?"

"This whole flirty bullshit thing we've been doing all these years. I'm done with it."

"What do you mean? You want me to stop flirting with you?"

"I want you to tell me how you feel. About me."

"Seriously?"

Callie says nothing.

"Well, I mean, you're gorgeous, Callie. You're funny. You're the greatest killing machine who ever lived. Your reflexes are—"

"Wrong answer!" Callie shouts, and clicks the phone off.

To Dani she says, "Thanks for helping me with that."

"My pleasure."

Callie takes a deep breath and lets it out slowly. Then says, "That's my goal: your complete and utter pleasure."

Chapter 30

CALLIE MOVES QUICKLY to the bed, traces her fingertips along Dani's thigh.

Dani trembles.

Callie taps Dani's wet spot lightly and says, "I think this area requires my immediate attention."

"I think so too," Dani murmurs.

"But first ..."

Callie lies down beside Dani, tilts her chin slightly upward, kisses her softly. Feels her pulse quicken.

Kisses her again.

And again.

Takes in Dani's sweet breath.

Hears herself make pleasure sounds.

Feels her cell phone vibrate in her pocket.

Ignores it.

Cups Dani's breast in her hand and slides her body lower until her mouth finds Dani's taut nipple.

"*Oh,*" Dani murmurs dreamily.

Callie's phone vibrates again.

She ignores it again, but thinks about it. Earlier tonight she made a mistake that could have ended her life. Not answering her phone could be even riskier.

Callie moves her hand downward until she finds the spot she seeks.

Dani gasps.

Callie's phone vibrates a third time.

She answers it.

Creed says, "You sound annoyed. And out of breath."

"Look, I'm—"

Creed says, "I'll get to it. Don't laugh, okay? The thing is I love you."

"What?"

"You asked how I felt and the answer is I love you, Callie. I don't just want us to work together. I want us to *be* together."

Callie jumps to a sitting position.

"Seriously?"

"Yes. Tell me you feel the same way."

"I do. I love you."

Dani, voice dripping with sarcasm says, "Well, thanks a *lot!* How nice for *you!*"

Creed says, "Who's that?"

"The TV. When can I see you?"

"I'll be there tomorrow at one, to meet with Sal."

"And after that?"

"Yes."

Chapter 31

"I'M SORRRY, DANI," Callie says. "I can't do this."

"I'm sorry too. And I deserve an explanation."

"We're in love."

"So I hear. You're about to be a couple. Like Sophie and I were this morning."

"Yes."

"Except that this morning when I was in a relationship with Sophie, you saw no problem sharing my bed. But now that *you're* in a relationship, it's a problem for you."

"What's your question?"

"My question is what's the difference?"

"The difference is this morning I would have said or done anything to get in your pants."

"Which means you're a lying, scheming bitch."

"I'll admit to that, given how things turned out."

"You didn't give a *damn* about my relationship with Sophie. You just wanted a conquest."

"Not true."

"No? You claimed Sophie was using me."

"I honestly believe that."

"Then tell me this: what makes you any better than her?"

Callie sighs. "Nothing. I'm actually worse than Sophie. But that doesn't mean she's good for you. On the other hand, Creed and I were meant to be together."

"I'd like to be happy for you," Dani says, "and maybe someday I will. But right now I'm too busy feeling like a complete fool."

"You're not a fool," Callie says. "You're the sweetest, most wonderful woman I've ever met. I feel terrible about this, because ..."

Dani waits.

Callie says, "Because you're everything I ever hoped to find in a woman. If Creed hadn't called I would have been thrilled to make a life with you."

"I've got a big, fat picture of that. We fall in love, move in together, start a life. Then one day Creed calls and you dump me. Because I'm your consolation prize."

"No. If we were already together, I would have told him no."

"I guess we'll never know, will we?"

"You won't. But I do."

Dani says, "Well then, I guess this is goodbye. Thanks for ... whatever."

"Dani."

"What?"

"I'm a part of Creed, and he's a part of me. As much as I want you, as perfect as you are, his call changes everything for me. I'm so very sorry."

"Yes," Dani says. "You most certainly are."

Chapter 32

Donovan Creed.
Sensory Resources Headquarters.

THE VIRGINIA COMPOUND will become Sensory East, and I'll build a Sensory West in Las Vegas with my own money. I'm not moving into Lou's old office. I'm happy with the one I've always had. It's comfortable and well-located. See that door on the left wall? That's actually an elevator that leads to my underground sleeping quarters.

I'm leaning back in my chair, feet propped on the desktop, sipping bourbon, basking in the warm afterglow of my phone conversation with Callie.

She didn't laugh.

She actually shares my feelings!

I think about our future together, sip some more bourbon. My cell phone vibrates. Caller ID says it's Dani Ripper.

When I answer she says, "My opinion? Callie came through with flying colors."

"Did you really test her limits?"

"I really did. I pushed as hard as I could."

I take a deep breath before asking, "How far did she go?"

"She was hanging in there really well until the phone call. What in the world did you say to her, anyway?"

I laugh. "I told her she was pretty, said she was a great assassin, told her she had great reflexes ..."

Dani laughs. "You're insane. First you concocted the whole 'Creed must be gay' routine, which is pretty narcissistic of you, if I'm being honest. Then she calls to ask how you feel about her and you tell her she's got great *reflexes?* Jesus, Donovan! If your intent was to throw her into my arms, it worked."

"That was my intent."

"Risky business," Dani says.

"Not as risky as marrying a younger, beautiful woman."

"You're planning to marry her?"

"Someday, absolutely. But I can't afford to fall in love with a woman I can't trust."

"Which is why you called me last week."

"Exactly."

Dani's a private investigator, but makes most of her money doing decoy work. Wives pay her to learn if their husbands are cheaters. Fiancés pay her to test their prospective husbands' integrity. Attorneys pay her to test the fidelity of their clients' spouses. Campaign managers pay her to test their opponents' characters.

I hired her to see if Callie was ready to enter into a monogamous relationship with me. I figured if she could stop short of having sex with a goddess like Dani Ripper, she'd be a good investment for my love. In my line of work, being in love's a luxury. I can't afford to take chances.

Dani says, "Well, she was everything you claimed, and more. Absolutely stunning! Prettiest woman I've ever seen."

"Did you see her naked?"

"Sadly, no."

"How far did she go?"

"You really want to know?"

"I need to know. That's why I hired you."

"Nothing happened before the phone call. After you shot her down, she was into it big time."

Dani pauses, waiting for me to speak. When I don't, she says, "We kissed."

"Did you kiss her first?"

"No. That wouldn't be honest. The target has to make the first move."

"Is that it? She kissed you? Nothing more?"

Dani pauses again. Then says, "She touched me."

"When you say she touched you ..."

"If you want me to be more specific, I'll need to bill you for two stiff drinks and a cold shower."

I chuckle, then say, "Did you touch her back?"

"No. Like I said, that's not part of the job."

"After I called her back and told her I loved her, did she stop immediately?"

"Yes."

"Completely?"

"Yes."

I smile. "And when she hung up, did you keep applying pressure to try to get her to continue?"

"I can honestly say I've never worked so hard to seduce someone."

"And she came through for me."

"She did. And I have the recording to prove it."

"Video?"

"You wish. Audio."

"Thanks Dani."

"You thanked me already, by keeping me out of jail last month. Not to mention the generous check you sent."

"Is there anything you'd like to add before we hang up?" I say.

"Two things. First, you've got a hell of a woman there, Donovan."

"I agree. And second?"

"If you hadn't called when you did, I would have surrendered."

"Surrendered?"

"By noon tomorrow, I'd have picked out an engagement ring."

"What would Sophie say about that?"

"Who cares? We broke up tonight."

"Oh. I'm sorry. I didn't know."

"It's okay. We're still going to be friends, still going to live together."

I'm confused. "Which part of breaking up am I failing to understand?"

"The sex part. It screws up friendships."

"You're sure about that?"

"Positive."

"Then do me a favor, okay?"

"What?"

"Don't say that to Callie!"

Chapter 33

TEN MINUTES AFTER Dani and I hang up, Callie calls.

"Did I wake you?" she says.

"No. Can't sleep."

"Me neither."

"What's up?"

"You think we can make it work?"

"Yes, of course."

"You've really thought this through?" she says.

I wait an appropriate time before saying, "What's on your mind, Callie?"

"All the things you'd have to give up."

"Such as?"

"The girlfriends. The hookers. The independence. The lack of accountability for your actions."

"I don't care about what I'm giving up. I care about what I'm gaining."

"You'll have to do something about Rachel."

"They'll never let Rachel out of the box."

"What about Beth?"

"How do you know about Beth?"

"I know about everything."

"Then you know Beth and I were never a couple."

"I know you tried. And I know she loves you. If we're together, that's a door you'll have to close."

"No problem."

She sighs.

"What's wrong?"

"I'm going to work hard not to be a bitchy, jealous girlfriend."

"That sounds promising."

"I'm going to try even harder not to interfere," she says.

I pause. "Are you about to interfere?"

"Yes."

"What's on your mind?"

"Miranda."

"Ouch. What about her?"

"Are you willing to give her up?"

"Sexually? Yes, absolutely. We've already agreed to that. But I hope you're not asking me not to hire her just because we were lovers."

"It was more than that."

"True. But at the end of the day, she was a hooker and I was a client. And I already promised her a job when she gets back from Europe next year."

"I know."

"She'd be a hell of an asset to us at Sensory."

"I agree. But as your girlfriend, it's my job to eliminate the competition."

"There's no competition, Callie. Tell you what. Miranda can report to you instead of me. Would that help?"

"Are you joking?"

"If I say yes will you believe me?"

"No."

"It wouldn't help if she worked for you?"

"Of course not!"

"Why?"

"Because every time I look at her I'll think about how you slept with her. And worry it could happen again."

"It won't happen again."

She sighs.

"You're willing to give it a try?"

"Probably. But I don't want her working with me."

"What if I station her here, at Sensory East?"

"You can't be serious!"

"What now?"

"You'll be traveling back and forth to Virginia all the time."

"So?"

"You'll go there alone. And stay for days at a time."

"So?"

"Days ... and *nights*. Think about it."

I pause, looking at it from her point of view.

"You see my problem?" she says.

"I do."

She sighs again. "I want to be the best girlfriend you ever had. I'll try to accept Miranda."

"We've got a whole year to decide what to do."

"True," she says. "And a lot can happen in a year."

"True. Wait. You're not thinking about killing her, are you?"

Callie says, "Not yet. I do like her. I just hope you don't cheat on me."

"You've got my word."

She laughs. "Say the whole sentence."

I laugh. "I give you my solemn word. I will never cheat on you."

"You really think you can be happy with just one woman in your life?"

"If that woman is you, I can."

"Thanks, Donovan. I needed to hear that. I'll be able to sleep now."

I say, "How about you? Are you willing to give up Gwen?"

"Yes, of course."

"When are you planning to tell her?"

"We'll tell her together, when we go back to Vegas."

"We? Why do I need to be there?"

"So you can explain she can't call you behind my back."

"You're pretty thorough," I say.

"Don't forget it."

"I won't. Any other concerns?"

"Just one."

"What's that?"

"We need a plan for tomorrow."

"You have something in mind?"

"A date," she says.

"Count on it. I'll be there at one o'clock. We'll spend a couple hours with Sal. After that we can go for a long walk along the river, and I can tell you about my plans for Sensory Resources."

"I'd rather hear about your plans for us."

"I thought we might get into that over dinner. Can we have dinner together?"

"If by dinner you mean room service, I've already got a hotel room."

"Perfect."

"Donovan?"

"Yeah?"

"We're not going to have a nice long walk along the river tomorrow."

"We're not?"

"No."

"Why not?"

"We'll be too busy having sex."

"Seriously? Okay, look. From now on you get to make all the plans for us as a couple!"

She says, "I'm telling you about the sex in advance, so you'll know it's a guarantee."

I laugh. "How did you come to that decision?"

"I flipped a coin."

"You flipped a coin to decide whether or not we'd have sex?"

"Yup."

"When?"

"The day I met you."

"God, you're special," I say.

"I'm guaranteeing the sex because I want you to be yourself tomorrow, and from now on. I love you, Donovan, and you don't need to be charming, witty, or flirty unless you feel like it. What I'm saying, I want our time together to be real."

"It will be."

"What I'm trying to explain is, you've already got me. I won't make you work for the sex. It's my gift to you, and it's yours for the taking. I want you to relax, be yourself, and know you're loved for no other reason than the fact you're you."

I think about what she said, and the meaning behind it, and respond, "That may be the most beautiful thing anyone's ever said to me."

"And I'm just getting started!" she says.

Chapter 34

Willow Breeland.
Las Vegas.

WILLOW STUDIES THE bald spot on the ancient head in her lap and briefly wonders how Carmine managed to upgrade the daily blow job to a full-service girlfriend experience. As he moves his head around she reminds herself to moan when appropriate, as he seems to prefer her low moan to the little gasping sound she usually makes when faking an impending fake orgasm. Thank God he isn't into the full-blown porn star scream, because her acting range is limited, and it would be embarrassing if the front desk called to complain.

"Mmm," she says. "Mmm."

"You like that baby?" he says.

What she likes is the after-sex talks they have, where she learns about his businesses and the people working for him. This is only their third day together, and to his credit, he's upgraded her from the fleabag motel she was in yesterday to a king room at the Venetian, with full room service and spa charging privileges.

"Mmm," she says. "Mmm."

Then—*oh, for the love of God!*—he starts motorboating her. He's buzzing her vertical lips with his horizontal ones, thinking he's driving her crazy.

She's got to nip this shit in the bud before he turns it into a regular feature. But how do you tell Carmine Porello he's a sexual moron without offending him?

"Honey, please don't do that," she says. "I love it, but ..."

"But what?"

"My boyfriend Bobby used to do that. I don't want to think of him, ever again. I want our time to be special."

"Bobby did that?"

"Yes. I'm sorry."

"But that's *my* move!"

"I'm so sorry."

"Shit!"

They're quiet a moment.

"I shouldn't have told you that." She says, with a sigh. "Look, it'll be okay. I'll try not to think about him."

"What? No way! I'm actually glad you told me that. But I swear, I could kill the bastard for ruining your pleasure like this."

"I know, and he was such a jerk, I'd turn you loose on him in a heartbeat. But like I said, someone else already killed him."

"Drug deal, right?"

"Right. Like I said, he's the only man I've ever been with. But ... can I tell you a secret?"

"Sure."

"You know what you were doing to me just before that? Down there?"

"Yeah?"

"It was making me crazy!"

He smiles. "You really like that, huh?"

"Far as I'm concerned? *That's* your move, baby!"

"Then let me serve up another round," he says, and does.

"Mmm," Willow says. "Mmm."

When Carmine rolls over, it's Willow's turn. When she's done, they lie on the bed together and snuggle.

"This is what I worked for all my life," he says.

"Me?"

"Yeah. You're my reward."

"I feel the same way about you," Willow says.

"Why?"

"I love your smile. And you make me feel safe."

He kisses her forehead.

She purrs.

He says, "I don't want you dancing at the club."

"Why not?"

"You're my girl. I want you to save this body for me."

"But you've been so generous. I have to earn my keep."

"You've earned it, believe me. And if we can keep meeting like this, well, let's just say you won't be sorry."

"But I want to help you."

"You *are* helping me."

"In your business."

He chuckles.

"What?"

"You're a child. What do you know about business?"

"I've got a wonderful business sense. And accounting experience."

"Accounting experience, eh?"

"Seriously."

"Well, I'm accounting on you to stay here and be happy. You've got your spa, your room service, cable, internet ... and me."

"You're in the best mood today!"

"I am. Wanna know why?"

"Yes, of course."

"Roy's dead."

"Roy?"

"That motherfucker finally got what's coming to him."

"And that makes you happy?"

"Ecstatic! But here's the twist. I didn't have nuthin' to do with it!"

"What are the police saying?"

"They're saying he got shot while trying to attack someone with a baseball bat. But he obviously picked the wrong guy, 'cause whoever it was put two bullets in him."

"Are you going after the guy?"

He says, "Can you keep a secret?"

"Better than anyone you ever met."

"I'll put the word out whoever did it needs to suffer. But secretly? I hope they don't find him. Because the guy who whacked Roy deserves a medal!"

"You think they'll find the shooter?"

"Yeah."

"Why, were there witnesses?"

"Not yet. But he apparently crashed into the guy's car, because there's paint transfer. They're looking for a burgundy car with the front smashed in. They'll eventually find it."

"You think they'll check the airport parking lot?"

"Yeah, sure. Why?"

"Because that's where I ditched the car."

He stares at her face a minute, then starts to laugh.

"You got me!" he says, grinning.

Chapter 35

Four Hours Earlier.

"ROY WILL BE at the club all alone this morning from at least nine to eleven," Willow says. "Then he'll head home to eat lunch and take a nap."

"Why would he be there so early?" Maybe asks.

Maybe is Donovan Creed's twenty-year-old daughter. She's also a paid assassin with a double-digit body count.

"He thinks he's meeting two new dancers, an hour apart. Nine-thirty and ten-thirty."

"You set him up?"

Willow smiles. "He'll be pissed when the first one stands him up, furious when the second fails to show."

"Fifty grand," Maybe says.

Willow looks at Gwen.

Gwen shrugs.

Hoping for a discount, Willow says, "I'd like you to consider this a long-term association instead of a one-and-done."

"There'll be more killing?"

"Almost certainly."

Gwen raises her eyebrows.

Maybe says, "The best way to insure a long-term relationship is to pay me what I ask each time."

"Yes, but fifty thousand's a lot of money."

Maybe shrugs and says, "According to Gwen, Roy's not just a mobster, he's a made man."

"He's not very dangerous. His right hand's in a cast!"

"That's why I'm only asking for fifty."

"Would you consider a counter offer?"

"I'm open to charging more."

Maybe's real name is Kimberly Creed, but why make herself a target for those seeking revenge against her father? A year ago she chose the name Maybe Taylor on a whim and has grown fond of it.

Willow says, "I'm only eighteen. Where am I going to get that kind of money?"

"You could charge people fifty grand for killing other people," she says. "That's how I do it."

Willow sighs. "Okay."

Maybe smiles. "Good. I'll need all cash, up front."

"You don't understand," Willow says. "I'm not going to hire you."

"You're not?"

"Nothing personal, but fifty's too much to pay for such an easy job. I should kill him myself. That'll impress Carmine more than hiring it out."

"Have you ever killed anyone? Because it might be harder than you think."

Willow pauses before answering, and not because Maybe or Gwen might be wearing a wire. The three women are nude, in a sauna, at the Venetian Spa.

Despite that, she sees no benefit in confessing murder to total strangers.

"Have I ever killed anyone? No. Can you give me some advice?"

"Kill him in his home, not the club."

"Because?"

"It's bad for business."

"Good point."

Maybe stands up, extends her hand. "Nice to meet you."

Willow stands, shakes hands.

"Thanks," she says. "Can I call you for the next one?"

"I don't see the point. The price would still be fifty. Twice that, if it's a big target like Carmine."

"I didn't say I couldn't afford you. Just that I can handle Roy by myself."

Maybe eyes her carefully. "Just out of curiosity, how much were you prepared to pay?"

"Ten grand."

Maybe laughs. "That's all you brought today?"

Willow nods.

To Gwen, Maybe says, "This one's thrifty. I think she'll make Carmine a hell of a good bookkeeper, if she can earn his trust."

Willow says, "Can you sell me a gun?"

"I suppose."

"How much?"

"Ten grand."

"*Seriously*, Ms. Taylor?"

"You could always pay some gangbanger five hundred for one that'll blow up in your hand. *If* he allows you to leave unmolested. *If* you trust him not to tell the cops he sold a gun to Roy's employee when he needs a get-out-of jail card. *If* you're not worried he might blackmail you for years to come."

Making a mental note to never again reveal how much cash she brought to a transaction, Willow says, "I'll buy your gun."

When Maybe leaves, Willow looks at Gwen and says, "Will you help me?"

"Kill Roy? No way!"

"Don't worry, you'll be miles away when it happens. I just need some tactical support."

"What do you have in mind?"

"We've both got long, blonde hair."

"Mine's lighter."

"In a ponytail, ball cap, sunglasses, same lipstick and eye shadow, and matching shorts ... we'll look enough alike to pull it off."

"Pull what off?"

Chapter 36

A COUPLE MONTHS ago, a rough character named Bobby Mitchell died while being treated for an accidental self-inflicted gunshot wound. Before that, he and Willow lived together in her apartment on Dillingham Drive, in Cincinnati.

Bobby used to boost cars by day, drive them to his uncle's chop shop on Carey Street, then snort the profits away while Willow lap-danced all night at the Firefly Lounge. Since Bobby was drunk half the time and high the rest, Willow refused to let him touch her car keys. Despite her best intentions, Bobby's proficiency at hotwiring cars left Willow without transportation on more occasions than she could count. Deciding this was a skill that could come in handy someday, Willow made him demonstrate his technique on her Toyota Corolla.

"Any idiot can hotwire a car," Bobby had said, "but if you don't know how to disconnect the fuel shut-off and steering wheel lock, you're not going to get far."

The skill didn't come easy to Willow, but she persevered, and eventually became an expert at hotwiring Toyota Corollas. She sold hers before moving to Vegas, but it's her car of choice. Since Willow hasn't had time to finagle a new car out of Carmine yet, she's still driving the Toyota she leased from Lyndon Car Rentals at McCarran International Airport.

Her plan for killing Roy is complex and relies heavily on Gwen's participation. It also requires her to hotwire her rental car in advance, so she can "steal" it from the valet parking lot at the Fashion Show Mall. In preparation, Willow disconnects the fuel shutoff and steering wheel lock, and creates a field between the terminals that allows her to crank the engine by simply passing a screwdriver through the field.

She drives to the Fashion Show Mall at ten o'clock, turns her keys over to the valet parking guy, and pretends to go shopping. In reality, she enters the notoriously slow Ruggles Department Store elevator, presses the express button for the Raintree Café, and performs a quick change, knowing two things. One, the Raintree Café isn't open till eleven, and two, the Ruggles elevator has no camera, a fact Gwen discovered three weeks ago when trying to report a speckle-dicked flasher.

When the elevator door opens on the third floor, Willow gets off wearing a black wig and hands Gwen the top she just removed, and the ball cap, and giant sunglasses. Gwen gets on the elevator, removes her black wig and puts on Willow's top, ball cap, and sunglasses while descending.

Meanwhile, Willow makes her way to the down escalator, heads to the valet parking area, finds her car, uses the screwdriver to crank the engine, and heads to the Top Six.

For the benefit of mall witnesses and security cameras, Gwen, dressed as Willow, will use Willow's credit card to do some light shopping.

Twenty minutes later, gun in purse, Willow drives to the Top Six, jumps out, and jams a large potato into the exhaust pipe of Roy's car. Then she drives two blocks, turns into an abandoned strip club parking lot, and backs her car against a telephone pole next to a junked bus. She puts the car in park, and waits. The good thing about Carmine's strip club, it's miles from the nearest residential area, which means it won't be hard to spot Roy's car when it passes by.

Moments later—much sooner than expected—she sees him coming. She ducks down to wait for him to pass, the idea being to follow him from a distance. When his car shuts down in a block or two, she'll be able to pull over, roll the passenger window down, and initiate a drive-by shooting.

But what she hears—and feels—is Roy's car crashing head first into hers. He's yelling her name. Something about seeing her sabotaging his car. She looks up and sees him pulling a baseball bat out of the back seat. Luckily for her, he's angrier than he is coordinated, thanks to the giant cast on his right hand. She grabs the gun, jumps out of the car, and carefully places two bullets into the center of his chest. Then she checks his tailpipe, but finds no potato. She puts Roy's car in neutral, then climbs back into her Toyota, puts it in gear, and pushes Roy's car out of her way. Then she goes back to Roy's car and puts it in park.

She notices the potato on the passenger side, grabs it, puts it in her purse, and drives to long-term parking at McCarran International airport. Once there, she waits in the car until she sees a family pulling their luggage across the parking lot. She files in close behind them and follows them to the drop off zone, where Gwen has been making circles waiting for her.

When she climbs into Gwen's car she says, "You've been at the mall the whole time?"

"Until twenty minutes ago."

"What did we buy?"

"You had a grande hot chocolate with skim milk at Starbucks, then walked around, spent some time in Vicky Secrets, where they're holding some cute undies for you. You also bought some soaps and bath salts at a store called Sea's Harvest. They're holding a green and blue bag for you, with a whale emblem on it."

"And the clothes, ball cap, and sunglasses you wore while shopping?"

"In the white bag in the back."

"You kept the sunglasses on at all times?"

"Yes."

"Even while signing the credit card receipt?"

"Especially then."

"Where did you change clothes?"

"Same place. Ruggles elevator."

"And you wore the black wig when you left?"

"Yes, of course."

"Thanks. Maybe we'll pull this off after all."

"You actually did it? You killed Roy?"

Willow doesn't think Gwen would tape her conversation, but you never know. To be on the safe side, she simply winks. Then she reaches into the back seat for the bag, and changes clothes before getting dropped off a half-block from the mall.

She walks back to the mall, retrieves the shopping bags from Victoria Secret and Sea's Harvest, then goes to valet parking and spends the next thirty minutes learning her car might have been stolen.

After the valet parking attendants have exhausted their search, Willow gets directory assistance on the phone, and has them dial Lyndon Rental Cars. When the Lyndon rep answers, the parking attendants hear her say, "Yes. I hope you can help me. It appears someone may have stolen my car ... Willow Breeland ... No, I don't have the paperwork. I left it in the glove box ... I'm staying at the Fairway Inn, here in town, but that's not where the car was stolen. Assuming it's been stolen ... This morning at ten I drove it to the Fashion Show Mall ... No, I used their valet service ... No, I'm still here ... Yes, of course they've been searching. You want to talk to the parking guy?"

She hands him the phone.

He talks a few minutes, then hands it back.

"Yes, I'd very much like another rental car ... What? No, I'll just take a cab ... Okay, thanks."

She hails a cab, catches a ride to the airport, repeats her story at the car counter, then gets her new rental, swings by her room at the Fairway Inn, takes a shower, and changes clothes.

Then she drives to the Venetian, to meet Carmine.

Chapter 37

Willow & Carmine.
Present Time.

"YOU KILLED ROY? Are you crazy?"

"I killed him for you."

"You're definitely crazy!" Carmine says.

"Crazy about you. I wanted to do something nice for you."

"Roy's a made man. If anyone finds out—"

"They won't."

"Your fuckin' *name's* on the car!"

"My rental car was stolen, far as the police know."

Carmine's taking it worse than she expected. She says, "Roy told some of the girls he was going to take you down. I couldn't sit by and let that happen. Plus, he threatened me."

"I *told* you to watch your step. He ain't right in the head."

"I know."

"You shot him?"

"Yeah."

"Where'd you get the gun?"

"It was Bobby's."

"The boyfriend? Wait. You didn't kill him *too*, did you?"

"Of course not! *Jesus*, Carmine!"

"Hey, I *had* to ask."

"I guess."

"And Gwennie helped you?"

"Yes."

"But how? You only blew into town how many days ago?"

"Four."

"And you met me three days ago."

"So?"

"Now you're hotwiring cars, killing made men, turning Gwennie into an accomplice. Next thing you know—"

"I hired Gwen."

"You what?"

"Hired her. To run the girls. For the Top Six."

"How the fuck?"

"I told you I've got a wonderful business sense."

"Gwen's going to run my girls?"

"Gwen and I are going to triple your business. If you'll give us the chance."

"How?"

"We've got plans."

"You're making me very nervous, young lady."

"Can I be frank? You're acting like an atheist at a Pentecostal convention. But think about it. Roy was your biggest threat. I got rid of him. Gwen coming back was your greatest wish. I got her for you. I was your greatest desire, and now I'm yours. Anything you want, anything you need ... you get. No matter what it takes. Just let me in, sweetheart. Let me into your business."

"You can hotwire a car?"

"Yes."

"Will you teach me?"

"If you're a good boy."

He leans over, kisses her breast.

Then says, "That took balls, killing Roy."

"You see any balls down there?"

"Not really."

"Maybe you should take a closer look ..."

Chapter 38

Donovan Creed.
Cincinnati.

THE PILOT TURNS and points a grim finger at the fighter jets on the runway.

"We should wait till they move, sir."

"Yeah, but I'm in a hurry."

"They're blocking the runway."

I'm running late because of some work I had the geeks perform this morning, and Callie just called to say she's on her way to the private airfield in Cincinnati to pick me up. Due to a faulty igniter, the jet I flew in on has been grounded. It's forty-five minutes to the nearest airport, and they don't have any private jets currently available for charter anyway. So I found an old Cessna 1SP in the hangar that can be legally flown by a single pilot. Since one of the private pilots has to stay with the broken plane, I hired the other one to fly me to Cincy in the Cessna. We wasted thirty minutes fueling and checking the systems, and now the fighter pilots are back on duty, sitting in their cockpits, twiddling their thumbs. They're not in my chain of command, which means they don't move unless the defense department tells them to.

Unfortunately, it's lunch hour at the Pentagon.

So here at Sensory, the fighter jets continue to sit at the far end of the runway, blocking our takeoff.

"You've got plenty of room, don't you?" I say.

"Technically, yes. But it's never a good idea to take off on a runway that's in use. I could lose my license."

"Those fighter pilots think they're hot shit," I say.

"They do indeed, sir."

"You know they're sitting there laughing at us."

"I expect you're right, sir."

I move from the cabin to the cockpit and strap myself into the co-pilot's chair and say, "What's your name, son?"

"James Rogers."

"What do your friends call you, Jimmy?"

"Buck, sir."

"Buck Rogers?"

"Yes, sir."

"I like that."

"Are you planning to fly us, sir?"

"No. But maybe it's time I asked you a question."

"Sir?"

"Who's the real pilot here, son? You? Or those guys?"

"Me, sir."

"Are you sure?"

"Yes, sir."

"Then let's show 'em what we're made of."

"For real?"

"You know you want to."

"I do. But you can't just go around doing whatever you want all the time."

"Of course not. But you can do whatever you want when your cause is just."

"What *is* our cause, if you don't mind my asking?"

"True love."

"Sir?"

"Can there possibly be a more noble cause?"

"Uh ..."

"Light the fires and kick the tires!"

"Sir?"

"Make them shit their pants, son."

"Yes, sir!"

He revs up the engine and taxis onto the runway. Then looks at me and says, "Aren't you even the least bit nervous?"

"Not at all," I say.

"Can I ask why?"

"Only three runways in the world make me nervous, Buck. One, Paro, in Bhutan, where only eight pilots in the world are certified to land, and even they can't do it without setting off all the cockpit warning sirens. Two, Matekane, in Lesotho, where the too-short runway suddenly ends at the edge of a 2,000-foot cliff and your plane is forced to plummet downward until it gains enough altitude to clear the mountain in front of you. And three, Barra International, in Scotland, where the runway is made of sand and disappears twice a day at high tide. These are tough runways, son. Not this one."

"But the fighter jets."

"We'll clear them with forty feet to spare."

As it turned out we cleared them with only twenty feet to spare. By then, Buck's drunk on the adrenalin rush, and we laugh and joke about the experience all the way to Cincinnati, where he touches us down safely, and taxis to our assigned drop off area.

I point at Callie's limo, entering the gate.

"There she is, Buck!" I say. "Wait till you see her!"

Buck brings us to a stop and winds down the engines. Then fusses with the old door till it finally opens. I descend the stairs to find Callie out of the car, running toward me. We have one of those Hallmark moments as we catch each other in a warm embrace, and share our first kiss.

And our second.

I'm going to pause here and freely admit I'm not an overly-emotional, touchy-feely kind of guy. So I'll spare you such details as the "surge of happiness" I'm feeling, and how "right" it seems, and how "time stood still" as we kissed, and all that crap. I'll keep to myself how my heart's pounding and do my best to refrain from all girly descriptions of how her lips seemed to hunger for mine, and how our passion "soared to heights unmatched by those who've loved before."

First of all, it wouldn't be true. I mean, how can I say you haven't felt the exact same thing when you kissed the man or woman of your dreams? What right do I have to suggest our first kiss was any more special than yours?

None.

I'll simply say that kissing Callie was the greatest feeling I've ever known, a moment I'll never forget.

It probably didn't hurt knowing in a couple of hours I'll be in her pants.

Chapter 39

CALLIE'S IN A sundress, I'm wearing a blazer and jeans, and holding a legal-sized folder when mid-west crime boss Sal Bonadello accepts us into his office. His face is ashen, completely devoid of the humor one can normally find playing around his eyes.

He's pissed.

Really, really pissed.

So angry, he doesn't flirt with Callie when we take our seats. This is a first, in my experience. I wonder if I underestimated his reaction to Frankie's death.

He points a finger at Callie. "*You* killed Frankie?"

"Yes, sir."

"On my orders, Sal," I say.

He keeps his eyes trained on Callie and says, "You live in Vegas?"

"Yes, sir."

"Nice place?"

"Nice enough."

"Carpet in your living room? Or hardwood floors?"

"Marble," she says.

"Marble," he repeats. "That *is* nice. What about your den?"

"I'm not sure I follow."

"Your den. Is it carpeted?"

She looks at me. I shrug. She looks back at him and says, "Yes, Sal. My den is carpeted."

"Tell me, my dear. What color is the carpet in your den?"

"Sage."

"Sage?"

"Yes."

"That's a color?"

"It is."

He shakes his head. "What is that, some sort of light brown?"

"It's more of a muted green, with greyish undertones."

"Greyish undertones," he says. "Sounds expensive." He pauses a moment, then says, "How much does something like that cost, ah—whatcha call—per yard?"

"I don't remember."

"No?"

"Not off-hand."

"But expensive, am I right?"

"I guess."

"You're not sure? Because it sounds pretty—whatcha call—impressive to me."

"I'd say it's definitely upscale."

"Sal," I say.

"Huh?"

"Are you okay?"

He looks at me through smoldering eyes and says, "Have you taken a shit today?"

"Excuse me?"

He checks his watch. "It's two twenty-eight. I was just wondering if you've taken your daily shit yet."

"And this is important to you because?"

"Because I haven't shit yet today. And I feel a huge one working its way through my colon."

We're two men looking at each other, one furious, one confused.

I finally say, "I hope you can hold it in till we're finished here."

"You'd like that?"

"If it's not too much to ask."

He looks at Callie and says, "I wonder if you'd be so kind as to lift up your dress so I can shit in your lap."

"I think not," she says.

"No? Well how about I fly to Vegas this afternoon, walk into your beautiful home, and take a big, fat, greasy shit on the upscale sage-green carpet in the middle of your fucking den. Would that be okay with you?"

"No."

"Really? Because you seem to have no problem taking my money for a simple hit, and shitting all over *me*! Maybe I've got too much respect. Too much—whatcha call—consideration. Too much decency. It's what prevents me from getting up from my desk, dropping my pants, and shitting in your lap."

171

"That, and the fact I'd kill you before you got your fly unzipped," she says.

"You're deadly in small numbers," he says, "In close quarters. I'll give you that. But I don't operate with small numbers. I don't play in close quarters. And *you* crossed the line."

"We had a reason for our actions," I say.

"Much as I adore you both, I'm—whatcha call—devastated by what you've done."

He slams his hand on his desk and yells, "Frankie was a *made man!*"

He slams the desk again. "A *captain!* My top earner!"

"I realize that."

"You realize that."

He looks at Callie and says, "He realizes that. I feel so much better."

To me, he says, "I'll require an explanation. And it better be the best fucking explanation I ever heard in my life, or I'll require—whatcha call—retri—retri—"

"Retribution?" I say.

"No."

"Remuneration?"

"Tribute. I'll require tribute. In the form of money and a life. Your money, Callie's life. And if you refuse to pay? We'll be more than enemies. We'll be at war."

He suddenly slaps the table again. "Because I *will* be respected!"

Slaps it again. "I *will* be consulted before you kill my people!"

"Are you ready to hear my explanation?" I say.

"Not yet. Three things, before you speak."

"Go ahead."

"One."

"Yes?"

"Put yourself in my position."

"What do you mean?"

"This lovely young lady sitting in front of me. Callie Carpenter."

"What about her?"

"She works for you. Reports to you."

"So?"

"She's got a girlfriend, yes?"

"For the sake of this conversation, let's say yes."

"I'm told her name is Gwen," Sal says.

"Leave Gwen out of this," Callie says.

"Please, dear. Hear me out while I speak to Mr. Creed. Because your life is literally on the line today."

To me, he says, "Suppose you paid me money—for whatever reason—to kill Gwen, but I take it upon myself to not only kill Gwen, but Callie as well. Without even *discussing* it with you. Is there any *possible* explanation I could give you that would be—whatcha call—sufficient? That would sit well with the others who work for you? Is there any explanation I could give that would satisfy *you* as to why I killed your top person? Anything I could say that would allow you to forgive me?"

"Only one."

"Then that's the explanation I better hear. And the second thing?"

"Yeah?"

"I hope you don't plan to tell me you killed Frankie because he would have been furious with me for killing his wife, and that he would have come after me, tried to kill me."

"Why wouldn't that be a good reason?"

"Because he personally approved the hit on Angie. Because his kids are grown and he had a new girlfriend he wanted to marry."

"I hadn't heard."

"It's true."

"Do tell."

"And third?" Sal says.

"Yeah?"

"I hope you don't plan to tell me you killed Frankie because you found out he and Sophie were dealing drugs. Because I'm part of that deal."

"You are?"

"Yeah. Now go ahead and give me your reason for killing the top person in my entire organization without my permission."

Chapter 40

I LEAN FORWARD in my chair and place the folder I've been holding on Sal's desk. He opens it and looks at the thin stack of papers.

"What's this?"

"The first page is a copy of FBI phone records documenting conversations with Frankie. The next twelve pages are certified transcripts of phone conversations between Frankie and Special Agent Robert Thorne, of the FBI. If you read those transcripts, I think you'll be stunned to see what he's already given the Feds."

Sal glances at the papers and says, "What's this last bit?"

"The evidence catalog."

"What's that?"

"The sheet that documents where the evidence is being held, and what type of evidence they have."

"What type is that?"

"Audio tapes of the phone conversations, for one."

"There are three listings for audio tapes," he says.

"The others are recordings Frankie made of private conversations with you."

"I don't believe it. Anyone could type this shit up."

"You think? Plus, why would I want to kill Frankie for free, other than to save your ungrateful ass?"

"Frankie was as loyal as they come. This here's bullshit. Unless you've got proof says otherwise."

"One of those tapes on the evidence sheet is a private discussion he claims you had in your basement last Memorial Day, when you gave him the order to whack the DiPietro brothers."

Sal looks like he ate a bad fig. "That's on tape?"

"It is. Apparently you also told him to torch the Jersey Icehouse restaurant, and gave him a date and time to do it. And it was, in fact torched on that day, at that time."

"The FBI heard that?"

"They did."

He closes his eyes. After a long time he says, "What's the other tape?"

"A meeting he says took place here in the office ten days ago where you discussed a hostile takeover of Carmine Porello's territory."

"Frankie said that?"

"He did. And gave them the tape to prove it. I can't believe you don't strip search your people before having these meetings."

He waves a hand, absently. In a defeated voice he says, "That would be disrespectful."

"So is ratting you out to the Feds."

Sal looks at me like a guy on a sinking ship, watching the last lifeboat launch without him.

"The Feds have all this?" he says.

"*Did* have all this," I say.

"What's that mean?"

"Permission to reach into my jacket pocket?" I say.

He nods. "You already been searched."

I remove two microcassette tapes, and slide them across the desk.

"Happy birthday, Sal."

"What's this?" he asks hopefully.

"I was called to Virginia yesterday. Emergency meeting with Homeland Security. For some insane reason they made me head of the whole anti-terrorist division. While I was there I thought I'd check out the FBI files on my good friend, Sal Bonadello. Imagine my surprise when I learned they had a full-scale investigation underway, based on the tapes and testimony of Frankie De Luca."

"These are those tapes?"

"Glance at the sheet in front of you that shows the location of the tapes"

"What about it?"

"There are tapes in those evidence cubicles. But one's Paul Revere and the Raiders, the other's Peter & Gordon's Greatest Hits. You're holding the originals."

Sal frowns. "You like that sissy music?"

"Who doesn't?"

Callie groans.

Sal looks at her and says, "I'm right, right?"

"You are," she says.

"What about the phone tapes?"

"They're in a different building. I couldn't get to them. But I had a friend erase them."

"How?"

"They were on magnetic tape."

"So?"

"He put a giant magnet in an envelope and stuck it in the adjoining cubicle."

He looks at me a long time, then calls Big Bad, his bodyguard. When Big Bad enters the room, Sal holds up the tiny tape and says, "We got anything here that can play this size tape?"

"Not that I know of."

"Yes you do," I say.

"What're you talking about?"

"When you patted me down you took my microcassette player."

"Oh yeah."

Sal frowns. "Go get it," he says.

When Big Bad comes back, Sal says, "Stay in here. I want you to hear this when I hear it."

He fiddles with the recorder a minute, then gives up and says, "I don't know how this shit works. You do it."

He hands me the recorder and one of the tapes and we listen to Sal telling Frankie to kill the DiPietro brothers. Then we hear some small talk. Then he tells Frankie how and when to torch the Jersey Icehouse restaurant. Then I switch tapes and we listen to the meeting where Sal decided not to support Roy in his effort to kill Carmine Porello because he heard I shattered Roy's hand and forced him to kiss Carmine's ring in front of the entire Top Six audience and staff.

When the tape ends, Sal says, "You heard all that?"

Big Bad nods.

"That's a tape Frankie made and gave to the FBI."

"Frankie done that? Naw, not Frankie! I don't believe it."

"You were in this very room when that discussion happened!" Sal says. "And the first one was in my own *home*, in the basement!"

Big Bad stares straight ahead, as if it takes him longer to hear things than the rest of us.

"There were only two of us in the fuckin' room," Sal says. "Me and Frankie. Unless you think I'm stupid enough to tape my own conversations and send them to the FBI."

"The Feds?"

"Yeah, that's right."

"Maybe the Feds bugged the office and your basement."

"Do you personally let Cheech in here twice a week to sweep my office?"

He nods.

"You ever see him find any bugs?"

He shakes his head no.

"And he sweeps my house the same days. It's not a fuckin' bug, it's a wire. Frankie made these tapes, and gave them to the FBI."

To me he says, "How much did they pay him?"

"You're not going to like my answer."

"Go ahead. Say it."

I shake my head, sorrowfully.

"How much?" Sal repeats.

"He did it for free."

"Son of a *bitch!*" Sal yells. "*Now* do you see why I told Creed to kill the bastard?"

Big Bad nods.

Sal says, "You heard the proof. Now tell the others what you know and tell them to shut their fuckin' mouths and let me run my own business. And never speak of this again. Frankie was a rat. You wanted me to kill these two today? Well this is why I'm in charge. It's why I make the important decisions and leave you to decide how many times you can pull your pud in the shitter while pretending to shit."

Big Bad looks at Callie. He's embarrassed. She shrugs as if it's no big deal.

Sal says, "Thank God for these two. Callie and Creed saved our asses. Again."

Chapter 41

"THANK GOD FOR these two?" Callie says.

"They saved our asses," I say. "Again."

"You have *got* to tell me what happened back there," she says.

We're in her limo, heading to her hotel so we can, *ahem*, do the deed.

She adds, "When Sal said he was in on the heroin deal I thought we were dead in the water."

"We would have been, but you saved us."

"How?"

"Last night you failed to create a backup plan to escape Frankie's closet."

"So?"

"It made me re-think our backup plan for explaining why we killed Frankie."

"Why?"

"My real reason for killing Frankie was to protect Sal. I thought he'd be furious at Sal for ordering a hit on his wife.

So that was the main reason, and you tortured Frankie so we could have a backup reason. But something you said last night made me think Frankie already knew Angie was getting whacked."

"Something I said?"

"You said it to Frankie."

"Tell me."

"After torturing Frankie a long time you said, 'You know what really pisses me off? You haven't even asked about Angie.'"

"Ah," she says. "He didn't ask about her because he assumed she was already dead. Because he knew I was there to kill her."

"That's what it sounded like to me. Plus the fact he lingered in the garage a while when she walked in the door."

"So the real reason was no longer a valid one."

"Right. So now the heroin deal became our reason for whacking him."

"Which left us without a backup reason."

"Exactly."

She says, "So how did you make all this happen overnight?"

"The geeks worked all morning on it. That's the reason I was late getting to Cincy."

"I understand that. But the geeks couldn't manufacture the tapes out of thin air."

"No."

She gives me an exasperated look. "So how did you manage to get the tapes?"

"I cashed in part of my life insurance," I say.

"Donovan."

"Huh?"

"This business about how you tell a little at a time to build up the suspense?"

"Yeah?"

"This shit needs to stop. You make me want to shove my hand down your throat to pull out the next word. Do me a favor."

"What's that?"

"From now on, when I ask you something, cough out the entire hairball at once."

"I've been taping Sal for years. I've got hundreds of them."

"How's that possible? You heard him. He sweeps his office for bugs twice a week."

I laugh. "Cheech comes in, runs a fancy wand around the rooms, tells Sal everything checks out."

"Why would he lie?"

"He's on my payroll."

She smiles. "You never cease to amaze me."

"Wait till we get to your hotel room!"

"Really?"

"Really."

"That's mighty big talk for an older guy. Is there something I should know?"

"Like what?"

"Are you hiding a monster in your jeans?"

"It's not the size of the sword that counts," I say. "It's the fury of the attack."

Chapter 42

"THE MOMENT OF truth!" Callie says, as we enter the room. "Are you ready?"

"Are you kidding? I've been ready for ten years!"

She laughs. "You've only known me for eight."

"Yeah, but I spent two years dreaming about meeting someone like you."

"And now you have. What's left unsaid? Anything?"

"Just this: you're the most beautiful, exciting woman I've ever met. And I adore you."

She sits on the bed, kicks off her shoes, and suddenly suffers a sort of winking spasm in her right eye.

"You okay?"

"Of course. Why, what does it look like?"

She does it again.

"Like you've got an eyelash caught in your eye?"

She laughs. "I was trying to give you a come-hither look?"

"Come hither?"

"A sexual rallying cry. A call to action."

"Do it again."

She does.

I say, "Got it. Next time I see it, I'll know what to do!"

"Wait," she says. "What if we're at a party and I actually *do* have an eyelash in my eye?"

"It would certainly liven up the party!"

"Perhaps a verbal cue would be better," she says.

She pats the space on the bed beside her and says, "Come hither, Romeo." Then adds, "How's that?"

"Works for me!" I say.

I kick off my shoes.

"Enough foreplay," she says. "Take me now!"

She lies down on her back in the center of the bed, spreads her legs, pulls up her sundress.

"What happened to your panties?"

She dangles them from her hand.

"When did you—"

"Do you really care?"

I sit on the side of the bed and lean over her, intending to plant a little kiss on her vertical smile when it suddenly happens.

An explosion.

Then a pause.

Then another explosion.

I'm so disoriented by the suddenness of the attack my brain is slow to react. But my body's in full fighting mode, circling, looking for attackers. But I see no one. I hear a gasp and turn toward Callie. See her eyes wide open, her face a frozen mask. Except for her mouth, which is opening and closing in a frightening way, like she's trying to get air, and can't.

I shout her name, and drop beside her on the bed.

She's trying to lift herself up, trying to speak.

I can't hear. My ears are ringing, mind's in a fog. I was so completely in the moment, and now we're in a different moment, and she's trying to speak. Trying to say something. I gather her in my arms and lift her up and see the blood. Not just some, but everywhere. Her back is sopping, the sheets beneath her drenched.

"Oh, *God!*" I scream. "*Callie!* Oh no! *Oh, my God, no!*"

Chapter 43

THE NEXT HALF hour's a blur. Even now, at the hospital, I'm having trouble remembering the exact sequence of events. I remember Callie passed out from loss of blood. I held a towel against her wounds, and called 911. Told the operator there'd been an explosion. Told her Callie's name, age, physical condition. Gave our location, Winston Parke Hotel, room three-sixteen. She told me to make sure the door was open, said someone would be with us shortly. Had me stay on the line, answer questions about Callie's condition so the medical team would know what they're dealing with.

"We're getting other reports of a bomb detonating," she said. "They're preparing to evacuate the building."

"Any other injuries reported?"

"Not that I'm aware of."

"Are you hurt, Mr. Creed?"

Was I? It never dawned on me to check.

"No injuries, I'm fine," I said. "Which tells me it wasn't a bomb."

"Apparently it was," she said.

"It was a gun."

"A gun? Are you certain?"

"Just a minute."

I pulled the bed halfway across the floor and looked through the hole in the concrete. It was a mess below us, but I saw a body, half-covered in dust and concrete, and the barrel of a giant handgun.

"Yes," I said.

"Sir?"

"It was definitely a gun. A handgun."

"And did you shoot your girlfriend, Mr. Creed?"

She said it in such a matter-of-fact way I almost didn't catch the question.

"What?"

"Do you have the gun in your possession at this time?" she said.

"The gunshots came from the room below us," I said. "The guy who shot Callie is lying on the bed in what I assume is room two-sixteen."

While keeping 911 on the line, I used my cell phone to look up and dial the hotel's number. When their operator answered, I put the room phone down and asked for the manager. When the manager got on the line I told him not to evacuate the building. Having all the people out front would delay Callie's medical treatment. I said, "Lock the exit doors, station a guard at each door, and let no one out. You're looking for a man or woman covered with plaster."

He said, "Is this a joke?"

I said, "What's your name?"

"Bruce."

"Pay attention, Bruce," I said, "because mine's the last voice you'll hear on this earth. Someone fired two very powerful shots below my room. Blew a hole so wide I can actually see the room below us. The rounds went through the ceiling, through my bed frame and struck my girlfriend in the back. She's seriously hurt. Ambulance on the way. The guy who fired the shots is dead. I can see him through the hole in the floor. If anyone was with him they'll be covered in plaster dust."

"First of all, you didn't move your bed," Bruce said. "Our beds are bolted to the floor."

"Do tell."

"Second, we've got a full-blown panic down here," Bruce said. "We don't have the personnel to station people at the doors, or the authority to hold our guests against their will."

"What type of security force do you have?" I asked.

"I'm not going to answer that question, since I don't know who you are. But the police have been called, and the sound you're about to hear will be us evacuating the building."

"No matter. It was probably one man, acting alone. And he's dead in the room below us. Here's what I want you to do, Bruce. Go ahead and keep the doors unlocked. But lock an elevator for the private use of the medical team that's on the way."

"What did you say your name was?" Bruce asked.

"Donovan Creed."

"Well, as we were speaking, I pulled the room record for three-sixteen. That room is registered to a Ms. Callie Carpenter. So it isn't "your" room, is it, Mr. Creed? In fact—"

"Don't even think about fucking with me, Bruce," I said, then noticed Callie had regained consciousness. She spoke in a voice so weak the only word I heard was "Donovan!"

I leaned closer. She coughed and gasped out some words.

What she said was, "I can't feel my legs."

I hung up on Bruce, picked the room phone back up, asked the 911 operator what was taking them so long. She demanded I stay on the phone with her, so I did, but used my cell to call my geeks. I told them what happened, and asked them to arrange a private jet to fly Dr. P. from Las Vegas to Cincinnati. Then I called Dr. P., told him where to meet the jet, and asked him what I could do to help Callie till the medics showed up. He asked me some questions about her condition, like, "is there an exit wound on her chest?"

"No."

"How's her breathing?"

"Shallow."

"Any blood or foam in the mouth?"

"No."

—That sort of stuff. Then he told me to run my fingernail across the bottom of her foot and see if she could feel it. But by then, Callie was dead.

Chapter 44

THE MEDICS SHOWED up and worked heroically to get her heart started, and managed to do so, but she died again in the ambulance, and again at the hospital. Each time they managed to bring her back to life.

"She's a fighter," one of the doctors said.

"No shit," I said.

They pulled her away from me and got her on a gurney and started wheeling her down the hall.

I yelled, "Don't die on me, Callie Carpenter! Don't you dare fucking die!"

"That girl's a fighter," one of the nurses said.

"You have no idea."

Now I'm in the waiting room, scared to death. Callie and I have been apart nearly three hours and no one's given me any information. The police have been in and out asking nonstop questions. They've researched me and learned enough of my legend to clear the waiting room and station half a swat team with me in case I decide to go Rambo on them, in which case they've been ordered to take me down.

Cincinnati SWAT is an impressive group. They're respectful, which I appreciate, and deadly, which I respect. At some point a police detective tells me the cops at the hotel believe they've got the whole story sorted out.

"You've just gone from suspect to witness," he says.

"What happened?"

"Classic love triangle. Guy named Ridley caught his wife cheating with Tom Bell."

"Who's that?"

"What planet are you from? Tom Bell? World champion contender? Mixed martial arts?"

I shake my head.

Detective says, "Ridley thought Connie and Tom were in room three-sixteen, so he got the room below them, intending to shoot them while in the act of sexual congress."

"Sexual congress?"

"That's what we call it."

I make a mental note to tell Callie. She'll like that. Sexual congress. Finally a congress we can endorse!

"What room were they in?" I say. "Connie and Tom Bell."

"They made a fuss at the front desk about not being able to get room three-sixteen. But as you know, it was being used. So they took three-fifteen, across the hall."

"Lucky for them, huh?"

He shrugs.

"What was so important about room three-sixteen?" I ask.

"It's Connie's lucky number. Her birthday, March sixteenth."

"Connie and Tom," I say.

He nods.

"What's Connie's last name?"

"I already said more than I should."

I nod. Then ask, "What about the gun? I never knew a civilian gun that could bore through concrete like that, though now that I think about it, the floor wasn't as thick as I would have expected."

The detective checks his notes. "Nitro Zeliska."

"What's that?"

"Make of the gun."

I make a mental note to tell Callie that, too.

Then I say, "You're telling me Callie might die because Connie and Tom Bell liked to fuck in Callie's room."

"No. If Callie dies it's because Connie's husband shot her."

He leaves first, then the SWAT team, and then I'm all alone in the room. I think about calling my daughter, but decide against it. She'll tell Gwen, and Gwen will insist on being here. I'd rather avoid that situation, and figure Callie would feel the same way.

Chapter 45

HOURS GO BY.

Dr. P. arrives, checks in with me, offers encouragement, starts to leave.

"Where are you going?" I ask. "You just got here!"

"I assumed you'd want me to check on Callie."

"They'll never let you in there."

"I'm a doctor."

"Not here, you're not."

"Donovan. I'm Eamon Petrovsky."

"So?"

"Go to the library sometime. Check out the books and articles written about me."

"Like what?"

"Oh, I don't know. How about *The Petrovsky Method?*"

"You're famous?"

"Among the medical community, I'm a god."

"You're a plastic surgeon."

"That face you're wearing? Have you forgotten I created that? No one on earth could have done that."

"Well if you're so fucking great, quit bragging and go save Callie."

"Any message you want me to give her?"

"Yeah. Tell her they'll never let you in to see her. Because you're a plastic surgeon, not a real doctor."

Dr. P. leaves the room in a huff, unaware I'm busting his balls. It'll make him work harder to get me the information I seek. I know he's got clout. He's not just the world's greatest plastic surgeon, he's Darwin. He understands bureaucracy. Knows how to cut through all the red tape. He'll meet the chief of surgery, don some scrubs, and gain admittance to the room where Callie's being treated. He's a legend in the medical community. If anyone can gain access to Callie and her treatment records, it's him.

A half hour passes before I see him again. When he enters the waiting room with another doctor in tow, I jump to my feet and ask, "How is she?"

"Donovan, this is Doctor Barnard, lead surgeon and Chief of the Medical Staff."

Dr. Barnard and I nod. Dr. P. says, "Let's sit."

"I need to know Callie's alive."

"She's alive."

I breathe a sigh of relief and take a seat. If she's alive, I can deal with anything.

Dr. P. says, "Brace yourself. Callie's paralyzed from the waist down."

Chapter 45

"I KNOW SHE'S paralyzed," I say. "She already told me. But it's a temporary condition, right? I've heard of this before. Temporary paralysis, caused by acute swelling. The swelling's impinging the spinal cord, or a nerve or something. When the swelling goes down, she'll regain full use of her legs, correct?"

The doctors look at each other. Dr. P. shakes his head and says, "I admire you, Donovan, always have. But you need to leave the doctoring to us. Because nothing you just said makes any sense. Nor does it accurately describe Callie's condition."

Dr. Barnard says, "Actually, one thing you said has merit. There is a single bullet fragment that somehow, miraculously, made its way between the spinal cord and the anterior spinal artery without severing either. Unfortunately, it's this tiny fragment that's causing Callie's paralysis."

"Can't a surgeon remove it?"

"The short answer is no."

"Why not?"

"It's a high-risk surgery."

"Why?"

"The fragment shows up as a speck on the MRI, which means there are probably numerous other fragments in the vicinity even smaller. This goes beyond microsurgery. There's a high chance a surgical procedure would do more harm than good."

"Why?"

"The surgeon could nick her spinal artery, or the spinal cord. One could kill her, the other could make her a paraplegic."

"But say the fragments *could* be removed. Would she be able to walk again?"

Dr. Barnard says, "That's the crazy thing. If the fragments could be removed, she'd almost certainly regain full use of her legs."

"She'd be as good as new?"

"After a sufficient recovery period."

"Years?"

"Weeks."

"Well, that's fantastic! Why the long faces? Why aren't we celebrating?"

Dr. P. says, "Because only a handful of surgeons in the entire world are qualified to perform this type of surgery, and none of them would dare attempt it."

"Why not?"

"As Dr. Barnard said, the risk of damage is too great. Callie's extremely lucky to be alive. Even luckier not to be a paraplegic."

"She's a virtual paraplegic now."

Dr. Barnard says, "Not true. Her actual diagnosis is paraparesis, a condition in which she has partial paralysis. Over the next few days she'll have increased, but limited use of her legs. While she'll never be able to walk again, she'll have some feeling in her legs. With extensive physical therapy, she could eventually hope to move them on her own, in a swimming pool."

"In a swimming pool?"

"It's not as grim as it sounds."

"Really? Because it sounds pretty grim to me! How many swimming terrorists do you know?"

"Excuse me?"

"Who's she going to be able to kill, a water aerobics instructor?"

Dr. Barnard appears uncomfortable with the direction the conversation has taken.

He says, "I'm afraid I don't follow."

"We need to find a surgeon who'll give it a try. Callie will take the chance. I guarantee she'll sign off on it."

The doctors look at each other.

Dr. P. says, "Donovan. The doctors won't do it because they're almost certain to worsen her condition. Their insurance carriers would never agree to the surgery, and no hospital would allow it to be performed for the same reason."

As he says this he gives me a wink. To Dr. Barnard it means nothing. An involuntary reflex, a facial tick. But to me it speaks volumes. Dr. P. held the same position at Sensory Resources that I've just agreed to take, but just as I'm also a free-lance hit man for the mob, Darwin had another job. He was Chief of Surgery at Sensory Resources. Our private hospital is full-service, with more high-tech equipment than any hospital in the country. Sensory is where spies go to get new faces. It's where I got mine, and where Dr. P. once supervised the implanting of a micro chip in my brain. It's also where presidents go to get checked out when they don't want the rest of the world to know what's wrong with them. If their medical issue turns out to be something minor, we ship them from Sensory to Walter Reed, and inform the public. We haven't had a life-or-death presidential situation yet, but if we did, the president would have the procedure done at Sensory Resources, and we'd keep his condition a secret from the media.

I thank Dr. Barnard for his time and ask, "When can I see her?"

"Let's give them twenty minutes to get her settled."

I nod.

"She'll be a bit groggy," he says.

"I like her groggy!" I say with more enthusiasm than Dr. Barnard expected.

He gives me an odd look, then leaves.

I'm excited at the possibilities, and quite pleased with myself for not killing Dr. P. when I learned he turned my daughter into a contract killer last year. I'd tell you more, but that's a whole other story.

"You'll do the surgery?" I say.

"Lower your voice," he whispers. "Here's the thing. We need to get Callie to Sensory Resources as soon as possible."

"Fine. We'll sign her out."

"These are civilians, Donovan. It doesn't work like that. They won't release her in her current condition."

"If her condition's that fragile, maybe she *should* stay here a few days."

"She can't. The longer we delay the surgery, the less likely it will be successful."

"Why?"

"A thousand reasons."

"Give me one I can understand."

"As the area around the bullet fragments heals, scar tissue forms. Then—"

I wave him off. "Never mind. We're wasting time. If I can kidnap her, get her to Sensory tonight, you'll do the surgery?"

"No."

"Excuse me?"

"This goes way beyond my training."

"You're the greatest plastic surgeon in the world."

"Thanks. The world happens to agree with you. But this is sub-dermal. Inside the body. You need a specialist."

He sees I don't get it yet and says, "I happen to know the world's greatest hand surgeon lives thirty minutes from this very hospital. But if you needed open-heart surgery, would you want her working on you? I hope not, because she wouldn't have the slightest idea where to start."

"Then what's your plan?"

He looks around before answering. As if what he's about to say might get him into worse trouble than suggesting I kidnap Callie. He says, "You won't need to kidnap Callie. You're the director of Sensory Resources. You have unlimited power."

"We're a clandestine agency. No one even knows we exist."

He smiles. "Your power comes from those who gave you the job. I'll teach you how to tap into their power to get any political door in the world opened, or any investigation closed. One well-placed phone call, Callie's on MedEvac to Virginia."

"Can I use that power to force a surgeon to do the operation?"

"No."

"Then what's the plan?"

"We need to get the best type of surgeon for the job."

"What type would that be?"

"After reviewing Callie's MRI films, I'm convinced we need a congenital/cardiothoracic surgeon. One who specializes in pediatric surgery."

"Pediatric? You mean a children's surgeon?"

"Preferably."

"Why?"

"They're uniquely qualified to deal with microsurgery."

"Are these guys hard to find?"

"The best in any field is always easy to find."

"So what's the plan?"

"We fly to New York, meet this guy, try to talk him into doing the surgery."

"And if he refuses?"

"You'll kidnap him and take him to Sensory. And this must be done quickly."

"Can I see Callie first?"

"Yes, but we're on a timetable here, Donovan. I can't stress that enough."

"Got it."

I call the geeks, update them on Callie's condition, ask them to arrange a jet copter to land on the roof of the hospital.

"No problem," Curly says. "Assuming you're talking about the remote control toy."

"What toy?"

"Jet copters aren't real, Mr. Creed. Did you mean a jet helicopter?"

"Yeah, whatever."

"What's your destination?"

"New York City."

"Bad idea."

"Why?"

"Average cruising speed, a hundred miles per hour. Two stops for fuel, you're looking at a ten-hour trip."

"How about a limo and a Lear Jet?"

"Three hours."

"Make it happen."

I click the phone off and say, "It's arranged."

He nods.

I say, "This guy we're meeting in New York City. He's the best?"

"Unquestionably. He's also the greatest pediatric heart surgeon in the world."

"You know him?"

"By reputation only."

"What's his name?"

"Dr. Gideon Box."

Chapter 47

"HI BEAUTIFUL!" I say.

"Hi Romeo," Callie says.

She's pale, her voice is slurred.

She says, "I'm so sorry, Donovan."

A tear trickles down her cheek.

"We've got a plan."

"If it involves kickboxing, you'll have to start without me," she says, forcing a weak smile.

"We're taking you to Sensory as soon as you're stable enough for MedEvac."

"Why?"

"We found a doctor who might be able to get you on your feet again."

Her eyes light up. "No shit?"

"No shit."

She sees Dr. P. standing behind me.

"Who's your boyfriend?"

"Dr. Petrovsky."

Callie frowns. "You're still palling around with Darwin?"

Dr. P. looks around, nervously. "Please, my dear," he says. "Let's refrain from using the D word."

"You trust him?" she says.

"Sometimes."

"Is this one of those times?"

"Yes."

"What do you need me to do?"

"Rest. Enjoy the drugs. But get stronger."

"You want me to multi-task at a time like this? Good thing I'm a woman."

"Why's that?"

"Women are better multi-taskers than men."

"Bullshit."

"You disagree?" she says.

"Of course. Men can have sex and a headache at the same time."

"The headache is an excuse. We say that when we don't want to have sex. You didn't know?"

"Doesn't matter. You've still proven me right."

She arches an eyebrow. "How so?"

"Men don't have to have sex, but when it's available, we don't want to leave it on the table. So if we've got a headache, or if there's a ball game on in the next room we can deal with the headache, listen to the game, and have sex, all at the same time. We're the ultimate multi-taskers."

"When it comes to sex."

"And football. And eating."

"I can't think of three things less important to a happy life."

"You just need the right dinner, the right team, and the right sexual partner."

"Any suggestions?"

She gives me her come-hither look.

I smile and give her a kiss.

She says, "You owe me a dance. Even if I'm in a wheelchair."

"At Sal's party you danced alone. I let you down."

"I agree. So how do you plan to make it up to me?"

"By doing everything in my power to help you regain the full use of your dancing legs."

"And if I do?"

"You'll never dance alone again."

"Say it better."

"From now on I'll dance with you every time you ask."

"For the rest of your life?"

I nod.

She laughs.

"What?"

"You *hate* dancing."

"But I love you."

"I appreciate your love. But don't start wearing a dress, okay?"

"Okay."

"Now quit hanging around," she says. "Go fetch my doctor!"

Chapter 48

DR. GIDEON BOX enters his office so briskly he doesn't see us sitting on his sofa.

Then he does.

Instead of being startled, he frowns and says, "Who the hell are you?"

"I'm Creed. This is Dr. P. We've come for a consult."

"I don't do consults unless they've been cleared by our advisory board. And how the fuck did you get in here?"

"We walked in," I say. Then add, "That's pretty salty language for a pediatrician."

"Pediatric surgeon," Dr. P. says, correcting me.

Dr. Box tries to correct me further, saying, "You didn't just walk in here. We've got security."

"You mean we're not really here?" I say.

"How about I call security, and let them sort it out," he says, reaching for the phone.

Before he can press the button to summon security, I've crossed the room and ripped the cord from the wall. I notice he's leaning on his desk, supporting himself with his right hand, fingers outstretched. I grab my knife from the sheaf on my ankle and quickly stab the desk between each of his fingers, one after the other, over and over, increasing my speed with each thrust.

When I stop, he says, "That's rather dramatic, don't you think?"

Under the circumstances, him being a world-class surgeon and all, I'd have to say Dr. Box is one cool customer.

"We've brought x-rays," I say. "I need you to take a look and give me your opinion."

"Fuck off," he says.

Dr. P. says, "We flew here from Cincinnati to get your opinion about a surgery."

"Round trip or one way?"

"Private jet."

"I'm impressed. But the answer's still no."

I say, "This patient is very important to me."

"Why should I care?"

I look at Dr. P. and ask, "Do we really need this guy?"

"I think so. Don't kill him yet."

"Who are you guys, really?" Dr. Box says. "Is this some sort of joke? Am I being secretly filmed? You, old guy: you look familiar. Are you guys strippers?"

Dr. P. and I look at each other.

Strippers?

I'm in my early forties, he's in his late sixties.

"I'll ask you again, nicely," I say, trying to sound nice. "I'd appreciate it if you look at these x-rays and MRI films and tell me if you have the ability to perform this operation."

"Tell you what," he says. "I'll thumb-wrestle you for it."

"Dr. Box," Dr. P. says. "This is Donovan Creed."

"So?"

"He's a government assassin."

"Doesn't mean he has thumb strength."

"He recently crushed the bones in a bouncer's hand like the man had rickets. He will absolutely break your thumb. If he does, you're of no use to us."

"George Washington," Dr. Box says.

"Huh? What about him?" I say.

Dr. Box reaches his hand into his pocket and pulls out a pecan.

"George Washington's the only man I've ever heard of who had enough thumb strength to crack a pecan."

"So?"

"If you can do it, I'll look at your x-rays."

"Toss it here."

He does.

I catch the pecan, study it, and frown.

"Something wrong, Mr. Creed?"

"This is made out of lead."

"In that case I guess we're through here."

Dr. P. tosses me his wallet.

"What now?" Dr. Box says.

I remove Dr. P.'s driver's license and hand it to Dr. Box.

He reads the name out loud. "Dr. Eamon Petrovsky."

Then looks at Dr. P. and says, "Never heard of you."

Dr. P. raises his eyebrows.

Dr. Box says, "Just kidding. You're my hero. Swear to God, I thought you were dead. Show me the films."

Dr. P. shows him the films and explains Callie's condition and situation using medical terms I can't begin to understand.

"What do you think, Doctor?" Dr. P. says.

"Child's play."

"Excuse me?" I say.

"This operation is beneath me. You'll have to get someone else."

"Are you fucking with me?" I say.

Dr. P. sees I'm losing my temper. He holds up a hand to stop me from doing something I might regret. He says, "Dr. Box, I'm told this is an impossible operation."

"For a dentist, maybe."

"No surgeon in the country will touch it."

"Typical," he says. "My *nurse* could successfully perform this operation."

"Would you do us the honor of giving Callie Carpenter the use of her legs?" Dr. P. says.

"You got a picture of her?"

"Excuse me?"

"Is she hot?"

I take out my cell phone and pull up a picture of Callie.

"Holy shit!" he says.

"Will you perform the operation?" Dr. P. asks.

"No."

"Why not?"

"The hospital will never approve it."

"Why?"

"You know why. It's too risky. There's not enough upside. Best case? She regains full use of her legs. Worst case? She dies."

"She'll take the risk," I say.

"Of course she will," Dr. Box says. "But the hospital won't. If it was a matter of life-and-death, maybe. But it's not. There's every reason to believe she could live another ten, twenty years."

"Ten or twenty? She's only twenty-six!" I say.

"Don't worry, she'll age pretty quickly from here on out."

"Suppose I can get the hospital's approval," I say.

"You'd still need mine," he says.

"Do you care to keep living?" I say.

"Not really."

"No?"

"What have I got to live for? I hate my job. I hate people, and they hate me. My girlfriend moved away and I'm about to lose the greatest surgical nurse who ever lived. I've ..."

"You've what?"

He smiles.

"What?"

"You're Donovan Creed."

"That's right."

"From Las Vegas."

"You know me?"

"I've heard your name before."

"Where?"

"I'll tell you another time. Unless you decide to kill me now. Speaking of which, nothing would make me happier than to have you kill me. I'd *pay* you to kill me."

"What're you, insane?"

"Possibly. Or maybe I'm too sane to want to keep living like this."

"I'll pay you a hundred million dollars to perform this operation."

"And if I refuse you'll kill me?"

"Worse."

He licks his lips, enthusiastically. "Tell me!"

"I'll kidnap you, rip off your nuts, sever your spinal cord, and make you spend the rest of your miserable life the way you're sentencing Callie to live."

"You're a rude personality," he says.

"You'd be wise not to forget that."

He says, "I actually believe you kill people for money. But you also torture them?"

"Sometimes."

"Are you any good at it?"

"I excel at torture. Why do you ask?"

"I've got a list of people who need to experience pain in their lives. And I'm tired of waiting for them to get sick."

"I have no idea what that means," I say, "but it sounds like we're about to forge an agreement, yes?"

"I hope so."

Dr. Box isn't shitting me. He goes to his computer and prints out a list. Twenty-two names with addresses, phone numbers, relatives, and personal notes.

"The people on this list have wronged me," he says.

"And?"

"I want them tortured."

"To death?"

"No. But thoroughly."

He pauses, then says, "And I want to watch."

Taken aback, Dr. P. says, "What kind of doctor *are* you?"

"A vengeful one," he says.

Chapter 49

I LOOK OVER Dr. Box's list.

"These are mostly housewives and clerks."

"So?"

"And your notes."

"What about them?"

I pick one of the names and start to read. "Chelsea Lloyd. Housewife. Married to Eugene Lloyd, sales rep, Commerce Real Estate. Laughed at me at Senior Prom."

I give him a look. "You can't be serious."

"She laughed at me. Made fun of the way I danced. Have you ever been singled out for ridicule among your peers?"

"No."

"It's devastating at that age."

"But you're a grown up. You're *past* that. You're a world-renowned *surgeon*! Meanwhile, this woman, Chelsea, is married to a sales rep."

"Your point?"

"We don't have to torture her."

"We don't?"

"No. We'll send her a copy of your press kit."

"I don't have a press kit."

"By this time tomorrow you will."

"How will you manage that? Elves?"

I start to deny it, then realize he's being facetious.

I say, "Success is the best revenge. My people will create the world's most impressive press kit and send it to all the women on your list. When they see who you've become, they'll shit."

"You think?"

"Absolutely. Not only that, they'll drive their husbands crazy reminding them how they could have married Dr. Gideon Box. They'll bring it up all the time. But every time they do, they'll remind themselves how badly they fucked up. That'll be torture enough, don't you think?"

"No. But it's a start."

"Anyway, here's the thing. It's not practical to torture people and let them live to tell the police. So we can either kill them, or we let it go."

He thinks a moment, then says, "Okay, here are my terms. One, you'll create press kits and send them to everyone on both lists."

"You've got another list?"

"Yes, of course. There are more than fifty names in all."

"You must have been the world's worst dancer!"

"They're on my lists for different reasons. You want to hear the rest of my terms, or what?"

"Go on."

"Two, you'll pay me the hundred million dollars you promised."

"Contingent on the operation being successful," I say.

"Same thing."

"Just to clarify, Callie regains full use of her legs."

"Of course. But I want the money held in escrow," he says. "With the attorney of my choice. Deposited today, before we leave."

"Banks are closed."

"First thing in the morning."

"Done."

"Number three, my surgical assistant, Rose, has to agree to come."

"Is she in town?"

"Yes, but she's hard to pin down."

"Fine. Surely that's it. I mean, you said the operation was child's play."

"Child's play for *me*. But I have one more demand."

I sigh. "Let's hear it."

"After Ms. Carpenter regains full use of her legs you'll fly back and have dinner with me and two guests at the place of my choosing."

"Locally?"

"A short drive."

"Me and Callie?"

"Just you."

"Who are the guests?"

"You'll find out at dinner. Not before."

"Should I be prepared for a physical confrontation?"

"No, of course not. This will be a civil dinner in a fancy restaurant."

"Of all your demands, why does this one concern me the most?" I say.

"Because it's beyond your control?"

He's right.

Dr. P. calls Dr. Barnard and asks if Callie is fit to fly.

"Absolutely not," Dr. Barnard says.

"What if we were in the field, under battle conditions?"

"No sooner than tomorrow morning."

"I'll have a MedEvac on your roof at six a.m."

"Without my cooperation," Dr. Barnard says. "Against my strongest recommendation."

"Noted."

Chapter 50

"TELL ME NOT be scared," Callie says.

"Don't be scared," I say.

"Tell me you'll be waiting for me in the recovery room."

"I'll actually be in the operating room with you."

"You'll do anything to see me naked."

"Damn right I will."

She smiles a lazy, drug-induced smile.

"I love you, Creed."

"Creed?"

"That's your name, isn't it?"

She goes out before I can answer.

Chapter 51

WE'RE IN THE operating room at Sensory Resources. I'm observing, Dr. P. and his old staff are doing their respective jobs in their supporting roles ...

... And then there's Rose.

If Dr. Gideon Box is a ten on the weirdness scale, his assisting nurse, Rose, is off the charts. Don't get me wrong, she doesn't act weird. Nor does she look weird. In fact, she's incredibly beautiful. So beautiful I catch myself constantly staring at her.

It's not infatuation.

It's fascination.

She's beautiful in a Walt Disney/Snow White sort of way, meaning her hair is jet black, her skin impossibly white, and her lips as red as rose petals. While she can't be more than thirty, when she looks at me, I feel a grandmother's love washing over me. I feel better in her presence, and I'm reminded of a young woman I met in St. Alban's Beach, Florida, who could take away your pain by standing near you.

Libby Vail.

Here's the weird part: just as I was thinking about Libby Vail, Rose says, "Donovan. Have you ever been to St. Alban's Beach, in Florida?"

"Huh?"

"You should check it out. I think you'd like it there."

"Shouldn't you be concentrating on Callie?"

"I work best when I talk."

"Why do you think I'd like St. Alban's Beach?"

"Your roots are there."

"What roots?"

"Ever heard of the pirate, Jack Hawley?"

"No."

"What's it been, three hundred years? Where does the time go?"

She smiles. "You used to look just like him."

Dr. P. and I exchange a look.

"How do you know what Donovan used to look like?" Dr. P. says.

"How do you know what Jack Hawley used to look like?" I say.

"He was your ancestor," Rose says.

"Of course he was."

She laughs.

"What?"

"You're just like him. No wonder Callie loves you."

I frown. "I'm just like a pirate? From three hundred years ago?"

She looks up, smiles, and there it goes again—grandmother's love.

"I used to climb onto a beam in George Stout's store and jump off, daring you to catch me."

"You dared *me?*"

"Jack Hawley."

"The pirate."

"Yes."

She smiles again.

Weird.

In a beautiful, Snow White, loving grandmother sort of way.

"We're done here," Dr. Box says. "Close."

"What? You can't possibly be finished," I say.

"Why not?"

"We've been here ten minutes."

"Look at the wall clock."

I do.

According to the clock, we've been here ninety minutes.

I think about what Rose said earlier.

Where does the time go?

Chapter 52

WE'RE IN THE recovery room. Callie's awake, on her side, slightly elevated. There are drainage tubes in her back. Rose is helping her drink some sort of smelly tea through a straw.

"What is it?" Callie asks. "Skunk cabbage?"

"Birch bark," Rose says.

She looks at me and says, "Like your great-great-grandfather used to drink."

"Who, the pirate?"

I wink at Callie.

Rose says, "Emmett Love."

"Who?"

Rose touches my shoulder, and my mind feels like it's flooded with images. Horses, guns, Indians—every western movie or TV show I've ever seen, I think.

Except in all those westerns I watched as a kid I don't remember seeing a dancing bear.

"Look up these names," Rose says. "You come from special stock."

"Right."

She suddenly flashes a stern look.

"Don't squander your heritage, Donovan."

"Yes, ma'am."

Did I just ma'am a thirty-year-old?

"You're beautiful, Callie," Rose says.

"You're the pretty one," Callie says.

"I do what I can. But you'd give Gentry a run for her money."

"Really?" Callie says.

"Really."

"Who's Gentry?"

Rose smiles.

When Callie's done with the tea, Rose runs her fingertips up and down Callie's legs.

Callie's eyes are focused on mine, which is how I can tell the moment she starts crying.

I touch her forehead. "Are you in pain?"

"No. I'm wiggling my toes."

Chapter 53

I HEAR VOICES me, celebrating.

"After all this time, we had to meet her," Curly says.

Larry waves at Callie. "You're my favorite," he says.

She waves back. "Thank you. I think."

C.H. says, "Hi, Rose."

"Hi, Charlie," Rose says.

He blushes.

Charlie?

This is the name that's supposed to be impossible for me to pronounce?

"You know my researcher?" I ask Rose. "How's that possible?"

"We met many years ago in the Florida woods," she says. "His family took care of me until I met the Stouts."

"Fine," I say. "Don't tell me."

I introduce the boys to Callie and say, "This is the first time they've left Geek City in years."

"Geek City?"

"It's okay," Curly says. "We named it that."

Dr. Box comes in and says, "Don't forget your promise."

"You've seen the press kit?"

"I have."

"And?"

"It'll do."

"We'll send it out today."

"What about our dinner?"

"The one with you and your mystery guests?"

"That's the one."

"Soon as Callie's back to normal."

"Fair enough."

"I don't know how to thank you, Dr. Box," Callie says.

"I enjoyed seeing you naked," he says. "Highlight of my career, in fact."

I frown.

Callie says, "You're not leaving, are you?"

"I've done my part, Dr. Petrovsky can take it from here."

"And Rose?" Callie says.

"I'll stay till you're on your feet," she says.

Chapter 54

Callie and Creed.
Sensory Resources.

TO KEEP GWEN at bay, Callie called her and said she had to assassinate a drug lord, and would be out of the country for eight weeks.

Gwen said, "You can't do that."

"Do what?" Callie said.

"Just come and go for eight weeks at a time without giving me notice."

"It's how the job works. You *know* that."

"Well, maybe I'm sick of your job."

"Meaning?"

"Maybe I won't be here when you decide to come home."

Callie said, "Do what you've got to do. But in the meantime, don't call me."

On day five Callie takes her first steps since the shooting. Her wounds are healing at a miraculous pace, and because she's convinced it's due to the birch bark tea, I ask Rose to teach me how to prepare it. She takes me to the woods, points out a stand of birch trees, and has me cut the bark strips. Then she shows me how to boil it.

"You should drink a cup every day," Rose says.

"Because my great-great-grandfather did?"

"That's right. And he lived to be a ripe old age. Considering the times."

"How did he die?"

"That's for you to look up."

"How is it you know so much about my ancestors?"

"How is it you know so little about them?"

I don't have an answer for that.

Then she says, "I've sent you two presents over the years. From the past."

"What are you talking about?"

"Think about it."

"I'm tryin' to think but nuttin' happens!" I say, imitating Curly, from the Three Stooges.

"One of the gifts is in your pocket as we speak."

I reach in my pocket and feel the silver dollar my grandfather gave me all those years ago.

"Unless you're my grandfather, I think you're wrong."

"Someone had to give it to him," she says.

Like I say, she's an odd one, this Rose.

"Where's the second gift?"

She frowns. "You squandered it."

"Do tell," I say, sarcastically.

"I sent you a cannonball."

I recall the cannonball. But it wasn't a gift. It fell from the sky during a horrific hail storm and crashed into the back of a truck I was sitting in.

... In St. Alban's Beach, Florida.

I look her over, carefully, and remember a hallucination I saw just before the cannonball struck. There had been a store near the truck. Through the rain I could barely see, but there appeared to be a young woman standing on the roof of that store, laughing. She had jet black hair, and eyes that glowed yellow, with a vertical black line in the center, like a jungle cat. If Rose's eyes looked like that, I'd haul ass and never look back.

But like I say, it was an apparition, something I imagined. Because when I blinked my eyes a single time, she was gone.

I don't recall telling anyone about the cannonball, but there were several men with me that day, and the guy who owned the truck kept it as a souvenir. If Rose has spent any time in St. Alban's, it's quite possible she could have heard about the cannonball.

And everyone who knows me knows about the silver dollar.

And there's this: she knows C.H., my elfin researcher. Charlie.

How's that possible? A woodland creature from centuries ago?

Obviously a bullshit story.

And yet it's clear they know each other from somewhere.

I think it over. Charlie's one of my top researchers. He certainly knows everything about my family tree. If he's been communicating with Rose over time, he might have told her about my heritage. My gut feeling says Rose isn't dangerous. She's grandmotherly, in a strange way. And yet I wonder if she's up to something. If so, I might have to find out the hard way.

How would it feel to torture someone who gives off a sweet grandmother vibe?

That afternoon, Rose leaves for New York. Callie and I finally find ourselves alone.

"Is there any such thing as too much love?" she asks, dreamily.

"I guess we'll find out," I say. Then add, "I know the true cost of love."

"Tell me," she says.

"Power."

She frowns. "Excuse me?"

"All love comes from power."

"You're serious?"

"I am."

"I've read a lot of romance poems," Callie says.

"You have?"

"Don't act surprised. But the sentiment that all love comes from power was never posited by Emily Dickinson."

"You're certain?"

"Quite."

"Should I explain?"

"Only if you wish to maintain the slightest hope of getting in my pants."

"That might actually happen today?"

"After our jog."

I smile. "Funny."

I start to speak, but she places her index finger over her lips and says, "Think this through, okay? Don't screw it up."

"Okay."

She waits a moment, then says, "Ready?"

"I am."

She nods. "Okay then. Say what you mean."

"Every drop of love you give costs a drop of your power. The more power you lose, the more vulnerable you become."

"What's the power *you're* giving up?"

"The power to not be hurt."

"You're saying the more you love someone, the more power you give them to hurt you?"

"Exactly."

"And that's why you don't fall in love easily."

"That's right."

"And this is all part of your abandonment issues?"

"Probably."

She looks down long enough to make me wonder what she could possibly be thinking. When she finally looks back up, there are tears in her eyes.

Lots of tears.

But there's something else going on in her face I've never seen before.

Hope.

"Are you okay?" I ask.

"Yes. Very."

She motions me closer, then slaps my face so hard it knocks me back.

"What the hell?"

Callie breaks into a huge grin and says "Omigod, Donovan!"

"What?"

"I just slapped your face! Again!"

"So?"

"You never saw it coming!"

"What, your hand?"

"A month ago you would've blocked that slap in your sleep."

"I've heard this before. What's your point?"

"You love me!"

"I already *told* you that! Are you going to keep slapping me every time you question my love?"

"Yes, absolutely."

"So even if I see it coming, I have to allow it?"

"You're the one who said that bullshit about giving me the power to hurt you."

She laughs. But there are still tears. She's laughing and crying at the same time.

"You love me!" she says. "You honestly, seriously, *love* me!"

I frown, thinking about the slap. "Try it again," I say.

She bursts into laughter. When it dies down, all that's left on her flawless face is her radiant smile.

"You love me," she says, "and it's okay."

"It is?"

"Uh huh. Because I love you, too."

"You do? Still?"

"With all my heart."

"What about Gwen?"

Callie laughs. "You need to work on that."

"On what?"

"Romance."

"What are you talking about? I'm romantic."

"Being romantic isn't the same as romance."

"It's not?"

She says, "I just told you I loved you, and you said, 'What about Gwen'?"

"It's a fair question. You're living with Gwen."

"What about your ex-wife, Janet?"

"What about her?"

"When you said you loved me I didn't ask, 'What about Janet?'"

"That's different. You *live* with Gwen. She shares your bed!"

Callie smiles. "Not after today."

She lets that comment hang in the air between us like a giant, heart-shaped balloon.

I reach for her hand and kiss it. Then slap her face.

"Ow!" She yelps. Then says, "I could've blocked that, if I wanted to."

Then she says, "What are you grinning at?"

I smile. "You love me too, Callie."

She rubs her cheek and smiles and says, "I know."

Chapter 55

Two Weeks Later.
Cincinnati.

"YOU DON'T LOOK like a claims adjustor," Connie says.

"No?"

"You look like a movie star."

We're sitting in Connie's living room, on her L-shaped sofa. She's on the sofa, I'm on the L-shaped section. Our knees are a foot apart. She's a bit over-dressed for the occasion, wearing an Alexander Wang V-neck sleeveless wrap dress, and black zip-front wedge sandals. I have no idea why she thinks a claims adjustor would be talking to her about her late husband's life insurance policy. All I said on the phone was I needed to get some additional information before the insurance company could pay the death benefit.

Whatever. It got me in the door.

"I said, you look like a movie star," she repeats.

"Thanks," I say, and throw a punch that catches her exactly where it was aimed, on her chin, effecting the exact result I intended, an instant knock-out.

When she comes to she finds herself naked, hanging upside down by her feet in her den. She screams, but the socks I've stuffed inside her mouth preclude her from making much noise. Nor can she spit them out, since I've placed duct tape over her mouth.

"I found a ski rope in your garage," I say. "I hope you don't mind me borrowing it. I didn't come in here with that thought, but when I saw this nice, sturdy beam in your den I figured it was the way to go. As for the nudity, you'll have to trust me when I say my many years of experience have taught me that naked prisoners are more cooperative than those wearing clothes. I know that sounds self-serving, but it's no less true."

She looks at me through wide, terror-filled eyes, and makes muffled sounds of protest.

I say, "Connie. Listen to me. I'm willing to lower you part-way, so you'll be more comfortable. Would you like that?"

She nods her head.

"Okay, then."

I adjust the rope until her back is resting on the floor, though her legs are still vertical.

"I didn't tie your hands on purpose, so please feel free to cover up whatever you wish."

She covers the parts I used to enjoy looking at before I saw Callie's. These days it's all business. Connie's body means no more to me than a slab of beef on a slaughterhouse meat hook.

"I'm willing to remove the duct tape on your mouth, and the socks, if you promise not to scream."

She nods.

I remove my knife from its ankle holster and say, "I'll hold you to that promise, Connie. Do you understand?"

She nods vigorously.

I remove the tape carefully, and manage not to tear her lips in the process. Taking the socks from her mouth triggers her gag reflex, which is rather gross, but it soon passes.

She says, "You *hit* me! You hit me and undressed me and tied me up! What kind of claims adjustor *are* you?"

"I'm not a claims adjustor, Connie."

"You're not?"

"No."

"Then why are you *doing* this to me? What do you *want?*"

"I'm doing this because seventeen days ago my girlfriend took two bullets in the back that were meant for you and Tom Bell. As a side issue, I could have also been shot, so for all intents and purposes, your husband attacked me. What do I want? Answers. Starting with why you cheated on your husband."

"What are you, some kind of religious freak?"

"Do I look like a religious freak?"

"No. But you don't look like a claims adjustor, either."

"As I said, I'm not a claims adjustor."

"So the company's not denying my claim?"

For reasons I'll never begin to comprehend, Connie has come to the conclusion I'm not planning to seriously harm her. She becomes—not comfortable, exactly—but somewhat relaxed, and conversational.

"Have you ever been married?" she asks.

"As a matter of fact, I have. But it didn't last."

"And have you never cheated?"

"Never did."

"What's it like being perfect?" she says, sarcastically.

"You think it requires perfection not to cheat on your spouse?"

She gives me a knowing look and says, "I bet your wife cheated."

"There's a happy thought."

"If we're going to talk a while, can you at least let me put my dress back on?"

"No."

"Is this how you get your kicks? Punching women unconscious? Stripping them? Tying them up?"

She's comfortable enough with my demeanor to transition from terrified to angry. Or maybe it's not my demeanor. Maybe it's this face Dr. P. gave me. I've always maintained the same demeanor when torturing women, and they always managed to hang onto their fear. Perhaps I should have Dr. P. add a terrifying scar to my cheek like I used to have.

Wait.

I can't do that.

Not without getting Callie's input first. It would be like her getting a Tyson tattoo on her cheek without asking me. I want to think about this some more, but Connie's working herself into quite a lather.

"You have the gall to ask *me* questions?" she says. "You want to know about my *affair*? My fucking *affair*?"

"Yeah, that's right."

"You *bastard!* You punched me in the *face!* Maybe I've got a question or two for you!"

"I'll entertain one."

"Oh you will, huh? You'll entertain one?"

"Is that your question?"

"My question, you sick pervert, is, *are you enjoying the view?*"

"You promised not to yell."

"No I didn't. I promised not to scream."

"Let's not split hairs. You'll keep your voice down or suffer the consequences. To answer your question, if you're referring to your nudity, no, I don't particularly care for the view. I mean, you're a very nice looking woman. But my interest in you has nothing to do with your body."

"You're sure about that? Because I could swear I caught you sneaking peeks at me."

"All pretty women think that. And it's possibly true. In the course of removing your clothes and tying you to the beam in the ceiling, I'll admit I noticed your body."

"Did it make you feel powerful? Like a big man? Ripping my panties off while I was unconscious?"

"Powerful? No. And you'll be pleased to know I didn't rip your panties."

"Be honest. You liked what you saw. And still like it. You wish it was yours."

I sigh. "Connie, I'm not a critical person. I think all women are beautiful. Having said that, I think you went too big on the implants."

"Oh, really?"

"Just my opinion."

"Anything else?"

"I feel you're past the age of being able to pull off the completely shaved look. Again, that's just me. I'm sure it worked for Tom."

"I think you're lying. I think you like the feeling of power. Seeing me naked makes you feel superior. Dominant. You're meek and small on the inside. The only thing you've got going for you is your looks. Your social skills obviously suck."

I pause a minute to look at my watch. Then say, "I'm sorry, Connie. I've allowed the conversation to get completely off track. Crazy as it sounds, you might be the exception to the nudity thing. It generally gives people a feeling of helplessness. But being naked seems to have empowered you."

I go to the bedroom, pick out a nightshirt, bring it back, hand it to her. As she puts it on I say, "I'm going to rethink the idea of stripping women from now on when I question them. I'll ask Callie what she thinks."

I can practically see the light bulb go off in Connie's mind. She's thinking Connie, Callie, similar names. Maybe she can transfer my feelings for Callie onto her, get out of this situation by warming up to me.

"Callie's your girlfriend?" she says.

Bingo.

The nightshirt can only cover so much while her legs are in the air, so I drape her dress between her legs and say, "I'll bring this to an end as quickly as possible. I'm trying to find out why Callie nearly lost the use of her legs. She could have been paralyzed for the rest of her life because you cheated on your husband. I guess I want to know if it was worth it to you."

"Thanks for covering me up. I'm sure Callie would be happy you did that."

I roll my eyes.

Connie says, "The short answer is yes. It was worth it. Not the part about Callie getting shot. If I had any idea that might happen, I would have gotten a divorce before dating Tom. But Ridley still would've tried to kill us. Apart from Callie being in the wrong place at the wrong time? Yes, the affair was worth it. Contrary to what you might think, I'm not a whore. I don't run around all over town, sleeping with men. I love Tom the same way you love Callie. And in your heart, I'm sure you know Tom and I had nothing to do with Ridley shooting her."

"I see it differently."

"Then why me?"

"Excuse me?"

"If you're being all self-righteous about my affair, why aren't you trying to string up Tom Bell? He's fifty percent of the problem, wouldn't you agree?"

"I wouldn't say fifty percent. You're the one who had the unstable husband."

"I didn't know he'd try to *shoot* us."

"Maybe not. But you must have known the affair would take a major toll on him emotionally."

"I honestly didn't think he'd find out."

"Because?"

"He's always so busy."

"With work?"

She nods.

"Is that your excuse? He was too busy? You wanted to be with him more, do things together, but he didn't have time for you?"

"No. The truth is I was glad he wasn't around more."

"Why, did he beat you?"

"No."

"Verbally abused you?"

"No."

"Was he a drug user? A drunk? A gambler? A control freak?"

She laughed. "Nothing like that. Ridley was a good man. A good provider. A supportive husband."

"But?"

"The truth? He was too fucking old for me."

Ouch. There it is, the answer I least wanted to hear. Because all this is really about me trying to understand why a woman like Connie cheated on her husband. If it was something he did wrong, some flaw in his character, I'd feel better about Callie and me and our chances for survival as a couple. You see, Callie and I share the same age difference as Ridley and Connie. And Connie didn't cheat on him because he mentally or physically abused her, or gambled, or drank, or anything else. She cheated on him simply because he was older.

"At what point did his age become an issue?"

"When mine did."

"What do you mean?"

"When I hit a certain age I saw myself on the verge of being middle aged. By then, Ridley was no longer getting the looks from women I'd seen him get when we first got married."

"But you were still getting them from men."

"Yes. And I needed them."

"You felt young around Ridley, but that didn't count. When other women saw him as being old, you saw him the same way."

"I suppose."

"At the point you decided Ridley was too old to excite you, you were open to being excited by another man."

"Now you sound like a psychologist."

"I'm disappointed in you, Connie," I say, looking at my watch.

"What's that supposed to mean?"

I reach for the socks and duct tape.

"You know what I think?" she says.

"What's that?"

"I think you're a coward. I think you took my clothes off to humiliate me, and I find it hilarious you came to my house to pick on me."

"Hilarious?"

"Yeah, that's right, big shot. You're a pussy!"

"You think?"

"A real man would've asked Tom Bell these questions. Of course, you obviously know Tom's a seventh-degree martial artist who could kick your ass from here to hell and back. So this is how you beat him. In fact, it's the only way a coward like you can beat a guy like Tom Bell."

"How's that?"

"By punishing me."

"That's an interesting theory."

"Tell me, big shot. How does it feel to beat up a woman half your size, strip her, hang her upside down, threaten and bully her?"

"Honestly? It feels pretty good."

"When Tom Bell finds out what you've done to me he's going to do the same to you, times ten."

"I don't think so."

"Why not?"

"Because I beat Tom to death before coming here."

Chapter 56

CONNIE SAW TOM as some sort of invincible being. To his credit, he was, in fact, a tough son-of-a bitch. I told her that, and said he gave a good accounting of himself, so she'd have a good memory of him. Nevertheless, she didn't believe I could possibly beat Tom Bell in a fair fight.

By way of proof, she said, "You don't have a mark on you!"

"Not true," I said, and rolled my sleeves up to prove it. "My fists are so swollen I can hardly close my hands. My wrists are sprained from the force of the impact, and my forearms are bruised to the bone."

"That's it?" she said. "I don't believe it."

"That's okay. I'm not trying to impress you."

"Why do you keep looking at your watch?"

"I'm waiting for it to be exactly three-sixteen."

Chapter 57

I DON'T JUDGE people. When I accept a contract for hire, I take the attitude my victim has already been tried, found guilty, and sentenced by the person paying my fee. It's easier that way, and prevents me from getting too wrapped up in "he-said-she-said" types of issues.

Likewise, I didn't kill Tom and Connie because they had an affair. Half the people you pass on the street every day are having affairs. What sort of person would I be if I went around killing all of them? And although I never cheated on my wife, I certainly cheated on some of my girlfriends.

Most of them.

Well, okay, all of them.

So I'm not entirely without empathy.

But I didn't kill Tom and Connie because they were cheating. I killed them because their affair set off a chain reaction that nearly cost Callie her life and the use of her legs. You can argue it wasn't Connie and Tom's fault, and I'd agree with you, to a point. I mean, had Connie fucked Tom at his house, the results would have been different. Ridley would have killed them both, or killed one of them, or Tom might have killed Ridley. In any case, the argument would have remained between those who were involved.

It's a matter of respect.

Rose says my great-great grandfather Emmett Love was a sheriff and saloon keeper in Dodge City, Kansas, in the eighteen-sixties. I'll bet if two cowboys got into an argument in his establishment he'd tell them to take it outside. Why? Because that keeps the argument between those who have a vested interest in the outcome. If they started shooting up the saloon, innocent people might get hurt. And I'll bet Sheriff Love wouldn't allow something like that to go unpunished.

I didn't punish Tom and Connie for fucking outside their marriage, but for failing to take their outside-of-the marriage-fucking outside.

You know, figuratively.

But they didn't. They took their affair to the Winston Parke Hotel, in downtown Cincinnati, and drew me and Callie into it. And right or wrong, you don't put my loved ones in harm's way without being severely rebuked. And you certainly don't expose my loved ones to possible death and live to tell about it.

Chapter 58

Six Weeks Later.
Top Six Lounge.
Las Vegas.

THE CLUB IS packed, the customers charged with anticipation. Carmine takes his seat. The house lights dim. The MC cues up the mike and says, "Our long-time customers will remember the greatest stripper in modern history, Vegas Moon, and how the Top Six flourished when she ruled the stage!"

The crowd cheers.

"Vegas Moon's real name is Gwen Peters, and now she's back, as a part owner! Gwen is now responsible for interviewing, hiring, training, and managing the Top Six girls!"

More applause.

"Gwen's kicked ass and taken names. No more three-piece band, or feedback mikes. She's put in a state-of-the-art sound system. Finest in the county! You'll get to hear it in a minute. And wait till you see the new light show! I swear it's like being at a million-dollar concert!"

He pauses. Then says, "But Gwen's made some other changes around here. Of course, you won't care about them unless you like gorgeous women."

The audience hoots and hollers.

"I've gotta tell you folks. I was backstage just now and I literally creamed my jeans! Gwen is in the fucking house! And she cleaned *out* the house! Remember Shirl, our nurse? She's the only one in the whole place who made the cut. Everyone else? Gone with the wind! I think you'll like what Gwen has done to Shirl's nurse's costume. Want to see it?"

The crowd calls, *Shirl-ee! Shirl-ee!*

The MC says, "Come say hi, Shirl!"

Shirl comes out wearing only a g-string, nurse's hat, and stethoscope, and the crowd shows their appreciation as she scampers off the stage.

The MC brings out the new girls, one at a time, each more beautiful than the one before. When they're all on stage, an electronic drumbeat starts, and the lights go out. A moment later, the lights and music synch, and twelve girls are suddenly doing choreographed moves that would impress the NFL's finest dancers.

Except that Gwen's girls are completely nude, except for their g-strings.

The crowd goes wild, and Carmine stands to take a bow.

Eleven girls leave the stage while one remains behind to dance. Every four minutes a new girl comes on stage, in her stripper outfit, and does a dance that ends with a few seconds of complete frontal nudity.

But the highlight of the night comes at the end of the show when Gwen takes the stage in a skimpy outfit to ask the crowd what they thought.

They loved it.

She tells them it's only going to get better from here on out, and says she'd like to introduce the newest member of Carmine's team, his new accountant, Willow.

Willow comes on stage nervously. The crowd can tell she's extremely shy. She's wearing glasses, a business suit, and has her hair pinched back in a tight bun.

The crowd offers her polite applause.

Then Gwen coaxes Willow to the center of the stage.

When she's there, Gwen says, "A little help please?"

Two of the dancers come out and grab Willow's wrists.

She yells, "What are you doing?" and tries to get away, but the other girls are too strong.

Gwen says, "I don't care how good you are with numbers. You don't come on *my* stage without getting naked!"

"No!" Willow shrieks, but the crowd turns on her like sharks on chum.

As Willow cries out, Gwen's girls come out one at a time and rip a piece of Willow's clothing off. The more they tear, the wilder the crowd gets.

Until Willow is down to her bra and panties.

The crowd is going insane. Shouting at the dancers to strip Willow.

Finally, one of the girls unhooks her bra from behind.

Willow shouts, "No!"

The crowd is on their feet, cheering the view of Willow's breasts.

Willow looks terrified.

Gwen looks mischievous.

Do it! Do it! Do it! The audience chants.

Gwen steps up to the mike and says, "Well, after all, she's an accountant, not a stripper."

She looks at Willow and says, "Unless you always secretly *wanted* to be a stripper!"

"No!" Willow says.

Gwen says, "They really love you, Willow, don't you boys?"

The audience cheers. They love her.

Gwen quiets them down and says, "Release her."

The two dancers release her and Willow puts one hand over her breasts, the other over her crotch.

"It's up to you, Willow," Gwen says. "This is your moment. Your once-in-a-lifetime. You could wiggle out of your panties for just a few seconds, and have the memory of getting the greatest ovation the club has ever heard. Am I right folks?"

She is.

The crowd's in a frenzy.

Willow appears torn. But it's clear she likes the applause. She slowly removes her hands, and tentatively shakes her tits.

An action that brings the house down.

When she steps out of her panties the audience loses it.

And Carmine's new accountant, Willow, receives the greatest ovation the club has ever given.

Afterward, backstage, Gwen says, "Nice call on the accountant strip thing."

"Thanks," Willow says. "It's a good start."

Gwen says, "I can't wait till we own the place!"

Willow winks. "I'm working on it!"

Epilogue

AT PRECISELY FIVE-FORTY my limo pulls up to 99 East 52nd Street.

"Wish me well," I say.

Callie kisses me. "Leave your phone on so I can hear. I'll be close by in case you need me."

"I doubt anyone would try to ambush me here, but–"

"But you never know. And anyway, I hate you being out of my sight, even for a couple of hours."

"Thanks."

"What if it's two women he wants you to meet? What if they're hookers and he's got a big evening planned for the two of you?"

"What would you do if that happened?"

"Kill him."

"You'd kill the man who saved your life?"

"I've already thanked him for that. Plus, he got to see me naked."

"Good point."

As I exit the car, Callie says, "If Rose is one of the guests, tell her I said hi."

"Will do."

I enter the door, climb the stairs that take me to a restaurant I haven't been to in years.

The Four Seasons.

Dr. Box is waiting for me in the lounge area.

"Ready?" he says.

I look around, checking for anything that seems out of place.

If something is, they've done a hell of a job, because I can't find it.

I follow Dr. Box into the Pool Room and scan the tables, but detect no one even remotely familiar to me. Eventually I see our destination is a table in the far corner. There's a woman seated there, with her back to me, sitting with a little dark-haired girl.

"Ladies," Dr. Box says as we approach, "I'd like to introduce you to my good friend, Donovan Creed."

The lady stands, turns, and extends her hand.

"Hello, Donovan," she says. "I'm so glad you could join us tonight. This is my daughter, Addie."

I take a deep breath and say, "Hello, Kathleen."

Personal Message from John Locke:

I love writing books! But what I love even more is hearing from readers. If you enjoyed this or any of my other books, it would mean the world to me if you'd send a short email to introduce yourself and say hi. I always personally respond to my readers.

I would also love to put you on my mailing list to receive notifications about future books, updates, and contests.

Please visit my website, http://www.DonovanCreed.com, so I can personally thank you for trying my books.

John Locke

New York Times Best Selling Author

8th Member of the Kindle Million Sales Club
(which includes James Patterson, Stieg Larsson, George R.R. Martin
and Lee Child, among others)

John Locke had 4 of the top 10 eBooks on
Amazon/Kindle at the same time, including #1 and #2!

...Had 6 of the top 20, and 8 books in the top 43 at the same time!

...Has written 19 books in three years in four separate genres,
all best-sellers!

...Has been published in numerous languages by many of the world's
most prestigious publishing houses!

Donovan Creed Series:
Lethal People
Lethal Experiment
Saving Rachel
Now & Then
Wish List
A Girl Like You
Vegas Moon
The Love You Crave
Maybe
Callie's Last Dance

Emmett Love Series:
Follow the Stone
Don't Poke the Bear
Emmett & Gentry

Dani Ripper Series:
Call Me
Promise You Won't Tell?

Dr. Gidon Box Series:
Bad Doctor
Box

Other:
Kill Jill

Non-Fiction:
How I Sold 1 Million eBooks in 5 Months!